SAILING  TO LOVE

He was sitting on the bed just behind her. His body barely touched hers, but it was enough to make her intensely aware that she was wearing only a thin nightdress. She wondered if he too was thinking of the fact that she had nothing on beneath it. And if so, did that thought tempt him? Did she sense a faint tremor go through his body? Could he sense the tremor in hers?

Perhaps he did, because he turned her gently so that she lay in his arms, her loosened hair flowing over her shoulders. He stroked it with light fingers before lowering his head so that his lips just touched hers.

She felt herself soften and grow warm under that kiss. It was gentle, tender, waiting for her response and suddenly she felt safe. Her hands seemed to find their own way, touching his face, his hair.

He drew back a moment to look down into her eyes, silently asking her a question.

She gave him her answer with a smile.

THE BARBARA CARTLAND PINK COLLECTION

Titles in this series

SAILING TO LOVE

BARBARA CARTLAND

.com

Barbaracartland.com Ltd

THE BARBARA CARTLAND PINK COLLECTION

Dame Barbara Cartland is still regarded as the most prolific bestselling author in the history of the world.

In her lifetime she was frequently in the Guinness Book of Records for writing more books than any other living author.

Her most amazing literary feat was to double her output from 10 books a year to over 20 books a year when she was 77 to meet the huge demand.

She went on writing continuously at this rate for 20 years and wrote her very last book at the age of 97, thus completing an incredible 400 books between the ages of 77 and 97.

Her publishers finally could not keep up with this phenomenal output, so at her death in 2000 she left behind an amazing 160 unpublished manuscripts, something that no other author has ever achieved.

Barbara's son, Ian McCorquodale, together with his daughter Iona, felt that it was their sacred duty to publish all these titles for Barbara's millions of admirers all over the world who so love her wonderful romances.

So in 2004 they started publishing the 160 brand new Barbara Cartlands as *The Barbara Cartland Pink Collection*, as Barbara's favourite colour was always pink – and yet more pink!

The Barbara Cartland Pink Collection is published monthly exclusively by Barbaracartland.com and the books are numbered in sequence from 1 to 160.

Enjoy receiving a brand new Barbara Cartland book each month by taking out an annual subscription to the Pink Collection, or purchase the books individually.

The Pink Collection is available from the Barbara Cartland website www.barbaracartland.com, via mail order and through all good bookshops.

In addition Ian and Iona are proud to announce that The Barbara Cartland Pink Collection is now available in ebook format as from Valentine's Day 2011.

For more information, please contact us at:

Barbaracartland.com Ltd.
Camfield Place
Hatfield
Hertfordshire AL9 6JE
United Kingdom

Telephone: +44 (0)1707 642629
Fax: +44 (0)1707 663041
Email: info@barbaracartland.com

THE LATE DAME BARBARA CARTLAND

Barbara Cartland who sadly died in May 2000 at the age of nearly 99 was the world's most famous romantic novelist who wrote 723 books in her lifetime with worldwide sales of over 1 billion copies and her books were translated into 36 different languages.

As well as romantic novels, she wrote historical biographies, 6 autobiographies, theatrical plays, books of advice on life, love, vitamins and cookery. She also found time to be a political speaker and television and radio personality.

She wrote her first book at the age of 21 and this was called *Jigsaw*. It became an immediate bestseller and sold 100,000 copies in hardback and was translated into 6 different languages. She wrote continuously throughout her life, writing bestsellers for an astonishing 76 years. Her books have always been immensely popular in the United States, where in 1976 her current books were at numbers 1 & 2 in the B. Dalton bestsellers list, a feat never achieved before or since by any author.

Barbara Cartland became a legend in her own lifetime and will be best remembered for her wonderful romantic novels, so loved by her millions of readers throughout the world.

Her books will always be treasured for their moral message, her pure and innocent heroines, her good looking and dashing heroes and above all her belief that the power of love is more important than anything else in everyone's life.

"Love always seems so far beyond the horizon, but it is really much closer than anyone imagines."

Barbara Cartland

CHAPTER ONE
1879

"The trouble with this house is that it was built for a family. Now there's only Miss Venetia."

The man's voice came from within the kitchen, and was answered at once by a female voice.

"It's her home. She wants it to be just as it was when her mother and father were alive. If you ask me, what she really needs is a husband."

Miss Venetia Baydon walked away quickly, fearful lest her servants should discover her outside the kitchen door and think she was eaves-dropping. She hurried to the drawing room, but found it as lonely as everywhere else.

It was late summer, the leaves were beginning to fall and a fine rain was drizzling down, lending a dull, bleak aspect to the grounds of Baydon Grange. Soon it would be winter, almost a year since her parents had died suddenly of pneumonia within days of each other.

The house was quiet and lonely, the more so because she was short of money and now had to make do with a bare minimum of servants. Johnson, the butler, his wife the cook and two housemaids were all she could afford. Most of her horses were sold and still she had less than she needed.

'How long before I have to sell the house itself?' she

thought. 'I couldn't bear that, yet I may soon have no choice.'

Mrs. Johnson had mentioned a husband in a way that made it clear she thought of Venetia as an old maid.

'I suppose that's what I am,' she thought wryly.

Twenty-four, unmarried with almost no money, she had little chance of marrying well now. Her only asset was her beauty. Her hair was a rich blonde, set off by eyes of sapphire blue and men had been known to sigh over her. But she knew that a sensible man cared more for a good dowry than a pretty face.

She was well-born. Her mother had been the daughter of a Viscount and her father the son of a Baronet, but a third son with no hope of the title.

As she grew up, she and her parents had travelled a great deal together and it had been a happy life, even though they never had enough money for people in their position.

They had worried about her marriage prospects, introducing her to eligible young men whenever they could. At nineteen she had received a proposal from an extremely handsome young man and had accepted it, believing herself to be love with him. But the man had cried off when he realised how very small her dowry was. He was in debt and needed a bride with a large fortune.

Venetia had wept briefly, and then forgotten him so quickly that she supposed she could not have been really in love at all.

Four years later she had accepted another proposal under her parents' urging.

"Darling I know he isn't handsome," her mother had argued, "but he's well-off and will give you a home. Besides, you're twenty-three and not getting any younger."

Reluctantly she had become engaged and stayed that way for three weeks. Then she had broken off the engagement, unable to endure her fiancé's long, dull speeches about himself.

"I'd die of boredom," she said to her outraged parents. "There has to be a more exciting way to live."

"Exciting?" her Mama echoed. "Marriage isn't supposed to be exciting. What will happen to you when we are no longer here?"

That had been last year and now they truly were no longer here. She faced a dispiriting future, yet even so, she did not regret breaking her engagement.

'I will wait for true love,' she told herself. 'And if it never happens, then I won't marry at all.'

She knew that she was unlucky in that her family had not exerted themselves to help her. But her Uncle Edward, the Baronet, had daughters of his own to marry off. He contented himself by inviting her to visit his London home occasionally.

She enjoyed these visits, as they broke the monotony of her normal routine, and enabled her to see something of her cousin Mary, who was only a year younger than herself.

It was the attraction of opposites. Venetia was cool, collected, intelligent. Mary was forgetful, scatterbrained, slightly irresponsible but utterly charming in a childlike way.

Sir Edward Wenmore Baronet, had managed to secure a minor position at court, and was intent on climbing the social scale as far as he could. He had inherited wealth from his father, married more with his wife, and purchased for himself a large, elegant property just outside the town of Windsor, near Windsor Castle, in Berkshire. He had explained this choice as being necessary for a man who must continually be ready to serve the Queen.

He had married two of his daughters well, and was putting all his efforts into securing an advantageous match for Mary.

Now the family was spending the summer in the country, at Wenmore Priory, and Venetia saw them now and then, but not often enough to stop her feeling lonely and isolated. She had often felt that she was not really welcome at The Priory. Mama had told her that it was because she was so much more beautiful than Mary, but then dearest Mama was biased.

Lost in these thoughts, Venetia failed to hear a carriage draw up outside and did not realise that she had a visitor until Johnson entered, saying,

"Miss Wenmore to see you, miss."

"Mary!" Venetia exclaimed. "How lovely to see you. I had no idea you were coming."

Mary ran forward and threw herself into Venetia's arms. Like her cousin she was fair, but whereas there was a richness in Venetia's looks, Mary's were pale, almost pallid. Her admirers called her fairy-like. Others called her insipid.

"Oh, Venetia," she cried, "I'm in such trouble and I don't know what to do about it."

Venetia stared at her with surprise.

Mary had never been a very emotional person. But now there was a note in her voice and an expression in her eyes which she had never seen before.

"What has happened?" she asked.

"I hardly know how to tell you," Mary said. "It's terrifying."

She was twisting her hands together as if they were somehow giving her the strength to speak.

"Papa has been to see the Queen at Windsor Castle."

Venetia nodded, remembering how Mary's father had always been very proud of being invited to Windsor Castle.

It was known to everyone that the Queen liked having men around her. She had a court of interesting and handsome men which, they all knew, helped to take her mind off the loss of her beloved husband, Albert. She had never recovered from his death.

"And did something happen there?" Venetia asked.

"Yes. I'm desperate, absolutely desperate. Perhaps the only thing I can do is to drown myself."

Venetia stiffened and stared at her.

"Nothing can be so bad as to make you want to die," Venetia told her.

"When Papa came back from Windsor Castle yesterday, he told me that the Queen wants me to marry her godson."

Mary's voice seemed to break on the last words and the tears were running down her cheeks.

"That must have been a surprise," Venetia replied. "But why are you so upset by it? Is he a terrible person?"

"I don't know. I've never met him. And it doesn't matter what he's like. I love – David."

"Who is he?" Venetia asked. "I cannot, at the moment, remember anyone called David."

"He is – the doctor's son at Coalville," Mary managed to gasp.

Coalville was a small town not far from her home.

Venetia now remembered a rather good-looking young man she had seen with Mary at one of the garden parties she had attended last year.

"He wants to marry me," Mary answered. "But he has only just passed his medical examinations. He has no money and not even a position at the moment. Papa wouldn't think him very important, while the man the Queen has chosen is the Earl of Mountwood."

Venetia drew in her breath, understanding at once.

As it happened she had heard of the Earl. A friend of

5

her father, with a place at court, he had visited them once, full of news of the latest scandal.

"It's Mountwood," he had said. "Decent fellow, always pays up when he loses at cards – not that he loses often. The trouble is he's too handsome for his own good, and can have any woman he wants far too easily. That is why he's never married, doesn't want to be burdened with a wife and so on. The Queen chides him for his disgraceful ways, but he can reduce her to jelly with a smile."

"But surely he needs an heir?" Venetia's mother had said.

"Of course, but I've heard him say that one day he'll marry anyone at all, just to have an heir. I don't think he means to give up his other activities, if you see what I mean."

And now the choice had fallen on poor Mary, who was crying helplessly. Venetia felt desperately sorry for her, as she suspected her situation was hopeless.

"I am sorry, darling," she said, "but I can't see how you can escape this marriage if the Queen is set on it."

"I have to escape it," Mary replied in a whisper. "Not just because I love David, but also because I think – I'm almost certain – that I am having his baby."

Venetia gasped. For a moment she could not believe what she had just heard. Her arms tightened round Mary. Then she said,

"How could you do that?"

"I love him," Mary sobbed. "I love him and he loves me."

Venetia drew in her breath.

She now knew that Mary truly loved David, but how he could have given her a child was beyond Venetia's comprehension.

Where could they have been that such a thing could

happen?

Almost as if she had asked the question aloud, Mary said in a broken whisper,

"We meet in a little house in the woods when it is cold and then he wants to kiss me. He makes it very comfortable with cushions and rugs and we are always so, so happy there."

'So happy,' Venetia thought, 'that Mary had surrendered to him. Now she was having his child.'

It all passed through her mind so that she felt almost breathless with the horror of it.

'How could she do such a terrible thing?' she asked herself.

Then almost as if she was being given the answer to her question she thought,

'Love is what every woman hopes to find. Love from a man whom she loves is something almost divine. After all, it was that knowledge that made me choose a single life rather than the wrong marriage.'

"Papa has everything arranged so that I have no chance to say no," Mary sobbed. "The Earl is coming to the house tomorrow night and the wedding will be the next day."

"The next day?" Venetia gasped.

"Yes, I'm trapped. Look – " Mary put her hand in her pocket and produced an envelope.

Opening it, Venetia saw that it was an invitation to the marriage of the Earl of Mountwood and Miss Mary Wenmore, two days ahead. It was true that Sir Edward was rushing his daughter into this before she had time to think.

It was monstrous.

"What am I to say? What can I do?" Venetia asked herself as Mary went on crying.

Then quite suddenly she knew the answer.

It was almost, she thought later, as if it came from Heaven itself.

In some strange way she could not put into words, she felt it was an answer which flew from the sky and touched her heart.

Her arms tightened around her cousin. Then she said,

"Now stop crying, we will find a solution to this problem. But we have to be very, very clever. One mistake and we'll all be beheaded or whatever punishment the Queen thinks appropriate for us.

"Now listen to me, Mary. We're going to save you from marrying a man you haven't even met and make it possible for you to marry the man you love, whose child you may already have in your body."

She thought as she said the last words that this was something she had never expected to happen to anyone she knew.

She would never have considered it possible for herself.

But as it had happened, and she was very fond of Mary however difficult it might be, she had to save her.

'And if she's carrying David's child,' she thought, 'how could she pretend to her unwanted husband it was his child?'

She took her handkerchief and wiped Mary's eyes.

"You need not marry this man," she said, "because I'm going to take your place."

Mary stared at her.

"You would make such a sacrifice for me? But how can you?"

"Because I have no one that I love or who loves me. And so *I* will marry this man chosen for you by the Queen. I only hope that in some way we will become friends and perhaps enjoy each other's company."

8

Mary gave a cry.

"But how can you be sure Papa won't guess that I'm not the bride?"

"That is where we have to be very clever," Venetia said. "You must pretend to agree to this marriage. Be charming to the Earl when he comes to your house."

"How can I do that when I hate him?"

"He is of no importance to you," Venetia said. "I am marrying him but if he's ghastly as he may be, I will at least not have a broken heart, as yours would break if you have to leave David.

"So you have to listen now to exactly what you have to do. It is the same as going on the stage. One mistake and the audience will laugh at you. Or, in this case, they will be very angry with you."

"I will do exactly what you tell me to do," Mary promised. *"Oh!"*

"What is it?" Venetia asked, seeing her stricken look.

"There's something I forgot to tell you."

"I'm sure there is. As long as I've known you, you've been forgetful and scatterbrained. All right, tell me the worst."

"As soon as the wedding has taken place the Earl has to go to India."

Venetia stared at her.

"India?"

"Yes, for about a year."

Venetia drew a long breath and spoke with ominous calm.

"Where in India?"

"A place called – um – the North-West frontier. I think. Or it might have been Calcutta. Or do I mean Delhi?"

"And you just forgot to tell me?"

"Well, I don't know anything about India," Mary said fretfully. "It's just – abroad, isn't it?"

"It's part of the British Empire. So I suppose it's still abroad. What is the Earl going to do when he gets there?"

Mary's eyes glazed and Venetia guessed that this was another detail that had escaped her attention.

"He's – he's going to be – attached to something," she said wildly.

"You didn't happen to find out what he's attached to?" Venetia asked patiently.

"It's to do with the Government – or he's carrying important documents – or something like that."

It was clearly useless to expect any more from her and Venetia gave up. Besides, a thrilling anticipation was growing inside her.

India.

The exotic East. Another world, thousands of miles away from her quiet little corner of England.

And she had thought she would never know excitement.

Now, all the excitement anyone could possibly want, was being handed to her. To refuse was impossible. This was fate.

Suddenly Venetia laughed.

"Very well," she said. "India it is. When is he going?"

"Immediately after the reception," Mary explained breathlessly.

"What?"

"He's leaving on the *Angelina*, a specially chartered ship that sails from Portsmouth that evening. We have to leave immediately after the reception."

Venetia gasped. Everything was rushing along much too fast for her. But she had said that she would do it and she could not back out now.

"Very well," she said. "I'll make a note of it."

"Oh, you are so wonderful," Mary said ecstatically. "The way you plan and organise things. I could never do it."

"That is undoubtedly true," Venetia said, rather amused. "How fortunate that you don't have to organise anything – otherwise the Earl might end up married to you, me, and probably your mother as well."

Mary giggled and Venetia was pleased to see her looking happier.

"But you simply must follow my instructions closely or we will be discovered." she added.

"I will do exactly as you say. But please come with me now so that you can stop me making mistakes."

"Come home with you?" Venetia questioned.

"Yes, after all you're invited to the wedding, and I'll say I wanted you to help me with my trousseau."

"Yes, it probably is better if I stay close by you," Venetia reflected. "Wait, I've had an idea. "If I have to go away to India with the Earl, this house will be empty. You must escape with your David while I am at the church marrying in your place and you two must be married at once. Then you must move into this house and live here."

Mary hugged her.

"You think of everything."

"I hope so. Now let's hurry upstairs so that I can pack."

Upstairs she packed all her very best clothes.

"Of course you must look smart when you arrive in India," Mary said.

"If I ever do arrive," Venetia answered with a smile.

"Of course the deceived bridegroom might drop me off en route or send me back by the first ship we meet which is returning home. Or I suppose he might just toss me over the side." She added cheerfully, "It'll be fun finding out."

"Oh Venetia, you're so brave."

"Well, you may have to be brave too because if he murders me I'll come back and haunt you."

It was when finally everything was packed in the carriage that Venetia took Johnson to one side and said,

"I am going to The Priory with Miss Mary and leaving everything in your hands. I might be away for quite a while. I've left some money in the desk to cover expenses."

On their way to The Priory they passed through a small village, where Mary stopped briefly at a shop.

"They take my messages to David," she told Venetia when she emerged. "I've asked him to meet me tonight in our place in the woods."

At last the carriage arrived at The Priory.

As the butler and two footmen hurried out to take their luggage upstairs, Venetia followed Mary into the drawing room.

Lady Wenmore was sitting at the writing desk. She got up when she saw Venetia had followed her daughter into the room and smiled as she heard Mary's explanation.

"How lovely to see you, Venetia," she said. "It's so kind of you to come and help."

Venetia smiled and responded politely, playing the role she had assigned herself. But she was thinking how much she disliked this chilly, haughty woman.

"I thought, with everything happening so quickly, you might need my help," she said sweetly.

Lady Wenmore smiled.

"My husband is delighted that Her Majesty should

have chosen such a charming and delightful husband for Mary."

Venetia longed to ask how it was possible to know he was charming and delightful when no-one had actually met the man in question. But she knew it was the sort of thing she should not say.

Upstairs in her room, they unpacked her clothes, and Mary said,

"Now I must slip out and see David, to tell him everything. I'll be back soon."

When she was alone Venetia did some thinking. Gradually more details of her plan were emerging in her mind. At last she went downstairs and sought out Lady Wenmore in the drawing room.

"I must speak to you," she said. "It's important. You know that Mary is unhappy about this marriage?"

"I know that the silly girl is making difficulties," Mary's mother said impatiently. "I'm happy to see that you have brought her to her senses."

"I hope so," Venetia said quietly. "But we are living more or less on a volcano. I feel that at any moment Mary will break down and have hysterics. I mean to prevent that if possible."

"I shall be very grateful. But how?"

"I feel it would be a mistake for Sir Edward to take Mary to the church. If he does so I think Mary will cling to him at the last moment and perhaps refuse to go ahead with the marriage."

Lady Wenmore gave a cry but did not interrupt and Venetia went on,

"I think it best for you and Mary's father to go to the church ahead and not to say goodbye to her. Just move away and she will know that you will be there when she arrives."

"But this is so unconventional," Lady Wenmore murmured.

"So is this whole wedding," Venetia could not resist saying. "We must take emergency measures to make sure that everything goes smoothly and the Earl is not insulted."

Lady Wenmore moaned at the thought.

"I will get her dressed," Venetia said. "She and the bridegroom must go to the church together. It's unusual, but we can't help that. If he is wise he will travel in silence."

"I will tell him that she is very nervous and very shy," Lady Wenmore said.

"Which is true," Venetia said. "I think also that it will be wise for you not to follow her and the Earl to the vestry where they will sign the register. Instead arrange for them to go there alone, and then leave immediately by the door at the back, where the carriage which will carry them back to the house will be waiting."

"You mean she won't walk back down the aisle on her husband's arm?" Lady Wenmore protested.

"I think you need to get her out of the church quickly, before she has too much time to reflect," Venetia said firmly.

"You are right, of course. I will tell my husband that he and I will go to the church in advance. We will make sure everything is arranged exactly as you want."

"Excellent. After all, we both want Mary to be happy for the rest of her life," Venetia said.

Then she hurried back upstairs to find that Mary had returned.

"Everything is arranged," she told her. "Your parents will go on to the church without you. The bride and groom will follow together. While we're all at the church you will make your escape with David."

"Thank you, thank you, darling Venetia," she cried.

"You are so kind and so understanding and I can only pray that you will not be punished for all this."

"I will be hoping the same," Venetia answered with a smile. "But don't worry about me. Just make sure that you and David vanish before they come back from the church."

"But what about the reception?"

"Neither the bride nor the groom will be there. I've made a new plan. The Queen is going to send the Earl a letter insisting that he depart immediately, without attending the reception."

"Is she?" Mary asked, wide-eyed.

"No, of course she isn't. I'm going to write it on Windsor writing paper. You told me your father had some in his office. Get it for me quickly."

Mary was back in a moment with several sheets of paper.

"There will be one letter to the Earl and one to your father," she said, "explaining why the bride and groom won't be at the reception. And a third letter to the Captain of the *Angelina,* saying that he must be ready to depart as soon as the Earl boards, which will be sooner than expected."

Venetia was already writing.

"There. Now it's done. Is there a servant you can trust to take this letter to Portsmouth tonight?"

"One of the footmen will do anything for me," Mary confided. "Give it to me, and I'll find him."

When she had gone Venetia sat down, wondering what on earth she was doing. Was she mad?

Well, it was too late to wonder about that now.

"It's done," Mary said, returning. "I gave him money for the train fare and he's on his way to Portsmouth. It's not a long journey so he should be back tonight."

"Then all that is left is for you and the Earl to meet this

15

evening. Be very careful what you say to him. In fact, say as little as possible. Try to sound shy but not in any way aggressive."

"I will be careful, I promise you I will."

"Then let us decide what we are going to wear this evening."

They decided on a soft pink gown that made Mary look demure. Venetia's gown was a deep blue satin that brought out the colour of her eyes. It was a year old, for she could not afford to replace it, but it made her seem elegant and fashionable.

At last they heard a carriage draw up on the gravel outside.

"Are you ready?" Venetia asked.

"I think so," Mary said in a trembling voice.

"Remember you have to act your part as if you are on the stage. Be quiet simple and charming. No one must suspect for a moment that we are arranging a revolution which will astound and eventually horrify everyone."

But although she sounded in command, the truth was that she felt very nervous as they descended the stairs.

Sir Edward was waiting with the Earl of Mountwood. There was another young man standing just in the background, but Venetia barely noticed him.

"Ah, my dear," Sir Edward said genially. "How pretty you look. Lord Mountwood, allow me to present my daughter and her friend, Miss Venetia Baydon.

The two girls sank into polite curtsies. Over her head Venetia was aware that the Earl was extending his hand to Mary, murmuring something.

Then it was her turn. She rose to her feet and found herself gazing into the eyes of the most handsome man she had ever seen.

CHAPTER TWO

Venetia realised that, until that moment, she had not seriously considered Lord Mountwood as a person. She had known a little about him from her father's friends, that he was a Lothario who made love to many women, moving easily from one to the other. She knew that he had resisted marriage in case it spoilt his pleasure. She had also heard that he was good-looking.

But as she looked at him now she discovered that nothing she had heard bore any relevance to the real man. He was, quite simply, overwhelming.

He was very tall and broad shouldered, with a commanding presence. He looked splendid in evening attire with a sparkling diamond in his snowy cravat. He looked as though he expected to snap his fingers and have the world dance to his tune.

Especially the female part, she thought wryly.

Then she noticed something else. Although he was smiling, there was a dark glitter in his eyes that spoke of danger. This was not a man to be trifled with and one to be wary of.

She began to wonder if her plan could possibly work after all. How would he take the deception? He might accept it with humour or his anger might be terrible.

But then Venetia felt a strange, new feeling go through her. It was so unfamiliar that at first she did not recognise it.

It was a thrill of sensual delight, something that no man had ever created in her before.

This man challenged her as nobody had ever challenged her in her life before. And something deep inside her rose willingly to the challenge.

"Miss Baydon?" he said, sounding slightly puzzled.

She realised that she had been staring at him and pulled herself together.

"Sir," she said demurely.

"It's a pleasure to meet you, madam," he said with a slight bow.

His eyes lingered on her in a way that she found disconcerting. Then he turned to the young man standing just behind him.

"May I introduce Lord Anthony Berwick, who is to be my best man?"

Lord Anthony was a willowy young man with a good-natured if slightly vacant expression. He greeted everyone pleasantly, but with very few words. He seemed happier standing in silence.

"My daughter has looked forward to this meeting, sir," said Sir Edward to the Earl.

"As have I," the Earl said. "I hope Miss Wenmore does not find me a disappointment."

Mary coloured and said hastily,

"Oh no, not at all."

"I'm happy to know that," he said.

His manner was charming, but Venetia wondered if she detected a fine edge of irony in his tone. He must surely be aware of how incredible this situation was, yet he seemed untroubled by it.

Then suddenly he glanced in her direction. For an instant their eyes met, and she almost gasped with the conviction that he could read her thoughts.

It was as though the two of them understood each other

and nobody else did.

"Dinner is served."

The butler's announcement came as a relief. With a flourish, Lord Mountwood offered his arm to Mary, who accepted it without fuss, Venetia was relieved to see. Sir Edward and Lady Wenmore followed, while Venetia and Lord Anthony brought up the rear.

Sitting next to him at dinner she discovered him to be rather shy. He was a young man of very few words – possibly because he did not know many.

"I think Ivan and Miss Wenmore look jolly good together," he said.

"Ivan? Oh, you mean Lord Mountwood?"

"That's right. She's very pretty, isn't she? She'll just suit him."

"But will he suit her?" Venetia asked, rather indignantly.

"Eh? Oh I say, yes. Of course he will. Rich as Croesus, you know. She'll have everything she wants."

"I should have thought that rather depended on what she wanted," Venetia observed.

"Well, all you ladies want the same, surely?"

"Do we indeed? And what would that be?"

"Well, you know."

"I don't know. Tell me."

"Well – " he repeated unhappily, "a title, plenty of money, a good husband – I say, I haven't said the wrong thing have I?"

Venetia relented at the piteous expression on his face. Being annoyed with Lord Anthony would be like taking shots at a baby rabbit. She was about to tell him not to worry when he sighed and said,

"I suppose I've said exactly the things I shouldn't say,"

he admitted meekly. "I do that a lot. Ivan's always saving me from situations."

"I can imagine," she said, her lips twitching.

"Always been a good friend to me."

"Were you by any chance at school together?"

"Oh yes. Eton. He stopped the others bullying me. Come to think of it, that's what he's been doing ever since."

"He sounds like a very good friend indeed."

"Oh he is. Mind you, he's got a devil of a temper."

"Has he?" Venetia asked uneasily.

"Oh yes. He won't stand for anyone taking liberties. His past is littered with corpses."

"Corpses?" Venetia echoed, startled.

"Oh, I don't mean literally. He doesn't kill people or anything – just makes them wish they were dead."

"You mean he's cruel and vindictive?"

"Oh, he's not cruel," Lord Anthony disclaimed eagerly. "But he's got the pride of the devil and he likes to be master. He won't tolerate anyone laughing at him, for any reason. But he's the best friend in the world."

"The best friend in the world as long as you always yield to him," Venetia said.

"Well, as I said, he likes to be master. He knows who he is and he knows what's due to him and woe betide anyone who forgets that."

A tinkling laugh from across the table made them both look over to where Mary was conversing with the Earl. Obviously he had just said something entertaining and Mary was playing her part well, regarding him with admiration.

"She looks just the kind of little wife he needs," Lord Anthony said.

"You mean meek and docile, and wouldn't say boo to

a goose?" Venetia asked. "But suppose she turns out to be different?"

"I say, I do hope not! I mean, he wouldn't like her answering back, or questioning his movements or – or – "

"Or minding about his other women?" Venetia said, looking him straight in the eye.

He turned so pale that she thought he was going to faint.

"I – I – I say!"

"He's notorious for them," she went on remorselessly. "In fact, rumour says that he's only marrying because the Queen picked out his bride and practically frog-marched him here."

"Yes but – I mean, nobody's supposed to – I say!"

"Of course nobody's supposed to know. Just as we're all expected to believe that he's going to be a faithful husband."

This time the hapless young man was beyond speech. He could only manage faint burbling sounds, indicative of complete horror.

"Are you all right?" the Earl asked, noticing his friend in extremis.

"Yes," Lord Anthony gasped.

"Something seems to have upset you, old fellow."

"No, no – nothing I do assure you."

"Lord Anthony and I were having a most interesting discussion," Venetia told him.

"About any particular subject, ma'am?"

"About character, sir. Personality. About how some people are easy to live with, some difficult and some impossible."

Lord Anthony made choking sounds.

"You got my friend to discuss all that, ma'am?" the Earl said admiringly. "My congratulations. I had not suspected him of such depths."

Lord Anthony recovered his tongue.

"It wasn't me," he said wildly. "It was her."

"That I believe," the Earl said gravely. His eyes were gleaming.

"That is – I mean – I say!"

Across the table the Earl's eyes met Venetia's and the look in them was the same, a look of pure, wicked glee. For a moment the rest of the world vanished as they were united in a joke that only they could understand.

"Won't you share your thoughts with us, old fellow?" the Earl teased. "I mean your thoughts on the subject of character."

Lord Anthony turned appalled eyes on him.

"Well," he said at last, "it's hard to – I mean – "

"Do not answer him, sir," Venetia said, laying her hand on his. "He's only trying to make fun of you."

"Oh yes, he does that all the time," Lord Anthony said abjectly.

"Well, don't give him the satisfaction. Lord Mountwood, my friend's thoughts are too deep to be shared with anyone, until he has reflected on them further."

Again there was that interchange of looks across the table, the wicked humour in his eyes and the invitation to share it with the same feeling that the two of them were set apart from the others.

"Very wise of you both, ma'am," he said.

Sir Edward's eyes were flickering suspiciously between them. He did not like the Earl paying attention to anyone except Mary.

At the end of the meal there were polite speeches. The Earl said,

"May my bride and I remember tomorrow as being the happiest day of our lives."

Sir Edward made a pompous speech about nothing very much and then they all adjourned to the library for coffee, where Lord Mountwood sought out Venetia.

"My congratulations, ma'am," he said. "Not many ladies could engage my friend in such sprightly conversation."

He was smiling at her and she could not help noticing how well shaped and attractive his mouth was. But she would not allow her thoughts to be reflected in her demeanour, which she kept severe.

"For shame sir, to mock Lord Anthony. How can you call him your friend and yet make him the butt of your humour?"

"You made him the butt of yours," he pointed out.

She was about to deny it when she recalled their shared amusement across the table. He read her thoughts accurately and gave her a teasing grin, saying,

"Poor Anthony was born to be the butt of someone's humour."

"Everyone's, you mean," she couldn't help saying.

"No, not everyone's. I tease him myself, but normally I would permit nobody else to do so. For you I made an exception, for I could see you were being gentle with him."

"Well, he's a very nice man," she said.

"He is, indeed. And you, ma'am, are also a very nice person."

He gave her a small bow and turned away before she could think of a reply.

The Earl had slipped his hand into his pocket and brought something out.

"Miss Wenmore," he said, "there is something I should like to say to you."

Mary turned nervous eyes on him.

"We are marrying under somewhat unusual circumstances," he said. "Our marriage is tomorrow, and our betrothal is today. Will you, therefore, please wear this betrothal ring?"

Without waiting for an answer, he took her left hand and produced the ring. Everyone watched, startled, as the largest diamond they had ever seen was slid up Mary's finger.

"This ring has been in my family for generations," Lord Mountwood said. "My father gave it to my mother, and on her death it became mine. I now give it to you, as my future bride."

"Thank you," she stammered.

He tipped her face up and laid his lips lightly on hers.

"Now we are betrothed," he said gently.

Mary was almost in tears, agitated by this development. Seeing that she was becoming flustered, Venetia murmured to Lady Wenmore,

"Mary should go to bed. She's becoming overwrought."

Because it was obviously the sensible thing to do, Lady Wenmore agreed with her.

"A charming gesture, Lord Mountwood," she said. "But now my daughter is tired and should go to bed, so that she can be at her best tomorrow."

The men inclined their heads respectfully. As Venetia bid Lord Mountwood goodnight his eyes flickered over her with a kind of careless ease that she found almost insulting.

Even she, inexperienced as she was, knew that he was assessing her as a woman, trying to strip away her clothes with his eyes. It was monstrous, she thought, that a man should behave in such a way on the night before his marriage.

Of course, Mary was a stranger to him, but that was all the more reason to treat her with respect.

She found herself feeling quite indignant on behalf of her cousin until she found herself remembering, with a jolt, that it was she herself who would be marrying him.

When they were safely in Mary's room, Mary let out a long breath.

"I was so nervous," she said. "I don't know how I got through the evening. Oh Venetia, what did you think of him."

"I'm not sure. I suppose we must admit that he is very good-looking.

"He is big and he frightens me," Mary answered. "I hated it when he kissed me. I don't want to be kissed by anyone but David."

It crossed Venetia's mind that she would not have minded at all feeling Lord Mountwood's lips on hers. Slightly shocked at herself, she tried to dismiss the thought.

"Yes, I don't think you would be at all happy married to him," Venetia replied thoughtfully. "I don't think he has a nice temper."

"Oh but then how will you manage if he shows you a nasty temper?"

"Don't you worry, I'll cope. I've got quite a temper myself."

"Take this," Mary said, pulling off the huge diamond ring as though it burned her. "I hate it."

Venetia took the ring, kissed Mary goodnight and went to her own room. There she undressed and lay in bed, staring into the darkness, wondering what was going to happen to her. The evening had left her astonished, excited and fascinated.

She had been warned about the Earl. He was the very last man in the world on whom she should be playing such a trick. His anger and insulted pride would be overpowering and she would be at his mercy.

Yet her courage was up and she knew she must not back out now.

'I can't let Mary down, after all my promises,' she thought. 'She must be allowed to marry her true love. If one really loves someone, it's impossible to switch one's emotions off. Love comes from the heart and whatever else we can force ourselves to change, the heart remains true to reality. It is impossible to alter what one feels in the very depths of one's being.

'So I can't turn back now. I refuse to be afraid of him, and who knows? Perhaps he'll find he's met his match in me?'

*

The next morning the whole household was in a bustle. Following Venetia's instructions Mary dressed in the bridal gown. Lady Wenmore looked in to say that she and Papa were about to leave. Lord Mountwood and Lord Anthony would arrive soon and travel to the church with her. She kissed her daughter and departed.

As soon as she was gone the two girls were galvanised into action. Swiftly they changed clothes so that Venetia was now the bride. Luckily they were the same size, and with the heavy veil concealing her face nobody could tell that there had been an exchange. Mary slipped away for a moment and returned in triumph.

"I've told the footman to change the luggage that is waiting downstairs to be loaded onto the carriage," she said.

"He's removing mine and replacing it with yours.

"And John is back from Portsmouth, where he delivered the letter to the captain of the *Angelina*. I've given him the letter 'the Queen' wrote to Lord Mountwood. He is going to give it to the best man when he arrives with Lord Mountwood and Lord Anthony will pass it on to the Earl. He'll give the other letter to Papa as soon as he returns from the church."

"Well done," Venetia said. "Listen, do I hear them?"

Mary looked out of the window to where a carriage had just arrived below. Inside it were Lord Anthony and the Earl, who looked up, saw her and waved. Greatly daring, she waved back.

"Did he see that you weren't in your bridal clothes?" Venetia asked anxiously.

"It doesn't matter. When you go down he'll just think that I changed very quickly."

"True. And since he saw you smiling at him, he won't suspect anything. Now, you know what to do. As soon as we have all driven away, you make your escape to David."

They looked at each other.

"I wonder when we'll meet again," Mary whispered, "and what adventures will have befallen us by then. Oh my dear cousin, I owe you so much."

They embraced warmly. Then there was a knock at the door.

"Lord Mountwood is waiting below for you, miss."

"I'm coming," Mary called. "Please go downstairs and tell Lord Mountwood that I will only be a moment."

Venetia was at the window, where she could see the Earl's carriage. Footmen were putting her luggage aboard.

It was time to go.

She had a last moment of panic. How could she be

doing something so reckless?

But then she saw Mary's face and knew that she must go on with it now.

They embraced each other again and Venetia left the room, walking slowly and carefully along the corridor and down the stairs. When she entered the hall, she saw a bouquet waiting for her on the table.

She picked it up and was aware as she did so that the outer door was open and she could see that her future husband was waiting for her.

As she left the house he held out his hand and she took it.

"So heavily veiled?" he asked, peering at her. "May I not see your face?"

She shook her head, dropping it a little so that it was impossible for the Earl to see through the veil, and pointing to Lord Anthony, to suggest that he was the reason for her extreme modesty.

She saw the footman handing the two letters to Lord Anthony, who received them with an air of faint bewilderment. Then he handed her gallantly into the carriage and soon the three of them were on their way.

"What's this?" the Earl asked, looking at the letters.

"This one's for you, the other is for Sir Edward," Lord Anthony said. A brilliant idea seemed to strike him. "I suppose I'd better give yours to you."

"That's an excellent idea," the Earl said gravely.

Venetia gave a faint choke of laughter which she instantly suppressed.

Lord Mountwood glanced briefly at her before opening his letter. She heard him draw in his breath as he read over the contents. Then he looked at her again, seemed to make up his mind about something and thrust the letter inside his jacket.

Venetia breathed a sigh of relief. It would have been awkward if he had wanted to discuss the contents with her now.

It was only a very short distance to the village where the church was situated.

As they drove along Venetia was aware that everyone by the roadside waved when they saw them.

"Now that the moment has come," the Earl said, "I hope you have no last minute doubts."

Venetia shook her head.

As if he thought she was shy and perhaps a little frightened of being married to a man she had only met the previous evening, the Earl said no more.

When the church came in sight, Venetia saw a crowd of village people waiting outside it. They cheered as the carriage drew up.

Then Venetia saw her Uncle Edward waiting for them at the Church door. She stepped out of the carriage, helped by one of the footmen.

Keeping her head down and her face hidden, she reached Sir Edward.

"Anthony – " Lord Mountwood said significantly.

"What – er – oh yes!"

He handed Sir Edward the other letter, triumphant at having performed his task.

"Let's go, old fellow," the Earl said.

They walked on ahead. Sir Edward stared at the letter.

"We must hurry," Venetia murmured.

"Yes, I'll read this later."

He took her arm and they moved quickly into the church.

Then he increased his pace as they moved towards the

altar. A glance showed Venetia that every seat was filled. There was quite a large choir sitting next to the organ.

There was a slight pause while they waited for the Earl and Lord Anthony to take their places, then she and Uncle Edward started on their journey down the aisle to where the priest was waiting for them.

She kept her eyes on Lord Mountwood, standing there, watching her approach, and it dawned on her forcibly how much taller and finer he looked than any other man there. Nobody else had shoulders so broad or carried himself with such an air.

At last she reached the altar and he came to stand by her side. The music ceased and the priest immediately began the service.

"Dearly beloved, we are gathered here today, to join together this man and this woman – "

Venetia had been to many weddings. She knew exactly what was happening without the need of a prayer book. But as the words of the service rolled over her, they seemed to have gathered a new and terrible significance.

"If either of you knows any impediment why ye may not be lawfully joined together in matrimony, ye do now confess it."

What could she say? That the bridegroom was being cruelly deceived?

In a firm voice the Earl made his promises, clasping her hand in his. Then it was her turn. The priest intoned,

"Wilt thou obey him and serve him, love, honour and keep him – forsaking all others – ?"

In a dazed voice she promised that she would do all this. She could feel her hand enclosed in his and no power on earth could have prevented her from promising to obey, serve and love him.

She wondered what was happening to her. She was almost dizzy.

When the priest blessed the ring which the Earl put on her finger, she felt as he touched her, that she somehow quivered, but hoped he was not aware of it.

He took the hand she extended, now wearing his diamond engagement ring and slipped the wedding ring onto it. Then he spoke.

"With this ring, I thee wed, with my body I thee worship – "

When they knelt and were blessed, the Earl put his hand on her arm.

He helped her first to kneel and then when they had both repeated the vows, he helped her to her feet.

He then offered her his arm as they walked towards the vestry.

The marriage service had taken only twenty minutes.

It was rather dark in the vestry and she had no difficulty in signing Mary's name and the Earl signed his.

Venetia was glad to see that her aunt had taken her advice and neither she nor her uncle came to the vestry with them.

As the bridegroom gave the priest an envelope which Venetia knew contained the money for the wedding and she hoped a large donation for the church, she moved towards the door, which the priest opened for her.

To her relief the carriage was waiting there, just as it should be.

Lord Mountwood helped her into the carriage and sat beside her. As they began to move out of the churchyard, Lord Anthony stood there, beaming with happiness for his friend, eagerly waving them off.

It was done.

CHAPTER THREE

As the carriage turned onto the road that led to the railway station, Venetia looked about her, as if puzzled, remembering that she was not supposed to know of the change of plan.

"You may wonder why we're taking this road," the Earl said.

It was the first time he had spoken to her since they had been married.

"Just a little," she said softly.

"I am afraid this will come as rather a shock to you, but the letter Anthony brought me contained orders from Her Majesty to proceed straight to the ship and not to the wedding reception. It seems she's had some information from India which has told her we are needed there as quickly as possible."

Venetia smiled to herself as she thought how carefully she had written those words. Then she replied,

"But of course we have to do what Her Majesty requires however difficult it may be."

She spoke in a soft, low voice which she felt he would not question. She had obviously been successful because he merely said,

"You are quite right and the sooner we get to India the better. It's only a short trip to the railway station and then we catch the train for Portsmouth. And now that we are man and wife, don't you think you could remove your veil?"

For a dreadful moment Venetia felt her mind go blank. Then a gust of wind saved her. Clutching her veil against the wind she said,

"Not in this wind. I must protect my complexion."

He gave a grin that, to her eyes, looked wolfish and said,

"Very well, madam. I'll wait until we are safely locked in the railway carriage."

And there was something about the way he said it that filled her with alarm.

At the railway station footmen hurried to take down their bags and load them onto the train. The first class carriage was ready for them. The Earl assisted her aboard, the whistle blew, and they were on their way.

For the first ten minutes they travelled in silence. Venetia was nervous in case the Earl should demand that she remove her veil, but he seemed absorbed in looking out of the window at the scenery.

'Almost as if I wasn't here,' she thought. 'If I was really his wife, I'd probably find that insulting.'

Then she remembered that she *was* his wife.

At last he said,

"It isn't a long journey to Portsmouth. We should be there in half an hour. Her Majesty's letter said that the Captain of the ship has been alerted to leave as soon as we board, and of course her word is law, which is why we are here and not at the reception."

Venetia inclined her head. "Naturally Her Majesty must be obeyed," she said.

"I hope you're not too disappointed at missing the reception?" he continued.

"We have more important business to pursue," she said dutifully.

"Indeed we have," he replied in a suddenly altered tone that sent a frisson down her spine. "A newly married couple always has important things on their minds. Is that not so?"

"I – yes – but – "

"But?" he echoed in a soft voice. "How can there be a but? What can matter more than – each other?"

"Nothing. But may I point out to you, sir, that we have barely met?"

"Are we any the less married for that? You knew the terms when you agreed to this marriage and you're just as much a stranger to me as I am to you."

"And we must both work to get to know each other – "

"Indeed we must. It would help if I could see your face. Come, this is excessive modesty. A new husband should at least be allowed to kiss his bride."

He had been in the seat facing her, but suddenly he moved swiftly so that he was sitting beside her, seizing her hands in his. Venetia gasped.

"You do agree that I may reasonably ask for that much?" he asked.

"I – yes, but – "

"Very good. Then we are in perfect agreement."

Before she could think of a reply, he drew her into his arms so that her head rested on his shoulder. For a moment he looked down into what he could see of her face behind the thin white silk of the veil, but he did not, as she had feared, try to remove it. Instead he lowered his mouth onto hers.

For a moment she was too astonished to react. The sensation of being kissed through her veil was unlike anything she had ever experienced before. It was mysterious and tantalising. She could not touch his mouth but she could feel its shape and sense how firm and mobile it was, how urgent and persuasive.

She was unable to do anything but cling onto him while unfamiliar sensations possessed her. She could feel his hot breath on her skin through the silk, and see his face looming over her in a way that was almost menacing, yet mysteriously exciting.

Whatever that excitement was she knew that it affected him too. His heart was beating hard enough for her to feel it against her own chest and his breath came swiftly. And, although she could not be sure, she had a feeling that his eyes were closed.

The next moment he muttered, "Damn this veil!" and swiftly pulled it aside. She was too overwrought to be alarmed. His lips touched hers with nothing between them. Now she had what she wanted, the touch of his lips directly on hers. She could feel their warmth and their firmness, but she sensed that behind them was an urgency and determination she had never met before.

She gasped at the fierce sensations that were coursing through her and pressed tentatively against him, seeking a respite. But there was none. He merely drew her more closely against him and intensified his assault on her mouth.

"Sweet," he murmured, "sweetness and honey – mine – all mine – "

"Wait," she gasped, becoming alarmed, "let me go."

He gave a soft laugh.

"I shall never let you go. You belong to me now – or at least, you will soon. In the darkness I shall make you mine so completely that your own self will become a stranger to you – "

Even through her inflamed senses she could feel a flicker of indignation. She did not want to lose her own self to any man. And he had no right to take such a thing for granted.

"I think I'd rather keep myself in my own possession," she managed to say, although it was hard to speak.

His reply was a laugh that vibrated through her, almost destroying her strength.

"That's what you think now," he whispered, "but when the darkness comes and I clasp your naked body against mine so that we become one, then you will be mine, completely mine. And I shall brook no argument."

He kissed her again before she could reply and for a while the sensuous pleasure that swamped her left no room for thought. How could she want anything, ever again, but to be drowned in such feelings?

But her true self would not be denied. She was an intelligent, thinking being and she could never give herself to a man who denied that.

"No," she gasped, beginning to struggle. "Let me go."

"I shall never let you go."

"Yes, you *will!*"

Exerting all her strength she managed to free herself from him just long enough to jump up and hurl herself into the opposite seat. He made to come after her, but stopped, his eyes fixed on her face with an expression of shock.

With horror she realised what had happened. He had ripped her veil away in a moment of passion so intense that he had been oblivious to her face. He had seen only her lips, covering them too quickly to be aware of anything else.

But it was different now. He could see her clearly and her deception was exposed to his angry gaze, long before she had meant it to happen.

"What the devil are you doing here?" he demanded in a voice of thunder.

Her mind went blank. What, after all, was there to say?

"Did you hear me madam? What are you doing here, dressed as my bride? And where *is* my bride? What have you done with her? Answer me."

Venetia glared back at him, trying to look braver than she felt.

"If you mean Miss Wenmore – "

"Certainly I mean Miss Wenmore. I don't have any other bride, do I?"

"Well – actually, yes, you do," she said cautiously. "You have me."

"Stop talking in riddles. Where is the woman I married today?"

"Sitting right in front of you," she said, recovering some of her spirit. "I was that woman, in the carriage, at the church, at the altar."

"And where is Miss Wenmore?"

"I have no idea," she said truthfully. "She slipped out of the house as soon as I had left it. By now I hope she is married to the man she loves."

He stared at her as though unable to believe his ears. Then he said sharply,

"Start at the beginning and tell me exactly what has happened."

"Mary has been in love with someone for a long time, but her father would not have thought him grand enough to be his son-in-law.

"Out of the blue she was told that she had to marry you and she was desperate to escape. So she came to me."

"I suppose it never occurred to her or to you to consult me."

"How could we? You had your orders from the Queen

and I doubt if you are brave enough to defy her. Mary even threatened to kill herself if she had to marry you."

"Then why the hell did no one tell me?" the Earl asked angrily.

"Because if she had done so no one would have listened. And you may as well know that she is having a baby by the man she loves. She couldn't possibly have married you."

"Evidently," he said curtly. "But I still say you should have got a message to me. I would have helped her to escape and talked my way out of it with the Queen."

"And risked her wrath?"

The Earl scowled at her.

"I'm not quite the milksop you seem to imagine, madam. I would simply have told Her Majesty that I arrived too late to prevent my bride eloping with another man. Even a Queen-Empress could have done nothing about that.

"Instead, the two of you invented this incredible farrago which might have been designed to make a fool of me. It's intolerable."

"I'm very sorry," she said. "But Mary was desperate to avoid you at all costs."

"Thank you!"

He was clearly in a terrible temper.

'I expect it is the first time,' Venetia thought to herself, 'that he's ever met a woman who wasn't flattered at the thought of becoming his wife. It'll do him a lot of good.'

"You realise what you've done?" he snapped. "We are now married. Tied to each other for ever."

"Perhaps not," she said, also becoming angry. She was rapidly deciding that the sooner this 'marriage' was ended the better. "After all, I used a false name."

"It makes no difference."

"We could ask to have the marriage declared null and void – "

"If you think I am going to let you make me a laughing stock over two continents, you are very much mistaken."

"You'll be that anyway when the facts are known," she was rash enough to say.

"But they are not going to be known. In a few minutes we'll be pulling into Portsmouth, where we will embark for India."

"And suppose I don't want to go to India?"

"You've left it a little late to decide that. You are now my wife and you will do exactly as I say."

"I most certainly will not."

He gave her a sardonic smile.

"May I remind you that only a few hours ago you vowed to love, honour and obey me? I may not have known who you were, but you knew exactly who I was when you made that vow, so I shall have no compunction about holding you to it."

"You can't want to be married to me," she said wildly.

"I don't. But I'm damned if I'll be laughed at. Do you understand? What did you think was going to happen when I discovered the truth? When were you going to tell me, by the way?"

"When the ship had set sail."

"So you meant to go through with it? Then why are you trying to get out of it now?"

"Because I had no idea what you were like. I thought you'd be – more reasonable."

He laughed aloud at that.

"You imagined you could play such a trick on me, expose me to derision and I'd just shrug and put up with it? Were you mad when you thought of that?"

"I think I must have been," she admitted. "But we still have time to put it right – "

"I've told you, you're going through with it. We are married and we are going to India. By the time we return nobody will remember that you were anything but the Countess of Mountwood, a title you will do your best not to disgrace."

"How dare you!"

"I dare because your behaviour so far has given me serious misgivings about your rearing. No young woman of my acquaintance would indulge in such a mad romp, putting herself in the hands of a man she knew nothing about. But it can't be helped. You are now Lady Mountwood and must remain so to the bitter end."

"The bitter end," she repeated in a hollow voice. "I wonder just how bitter that end will be."

"That depends on you. Learn to behave yourself as a docile, obedient wife and you won't find me too difficult to live with. But there must be no more such pranks. I won't tolerate that."

"You talk as though I was a slave, not a wife," she cried.

He shrugged.

"There's very little difference in the eyes of the law. You have made yourself my property, to do with as I please. If you don't like that prospect, you shouldn't have done it. You chose this situation, but from now on the choices will be mine."

She stared at him in horror as the full import of these words sunk in. What he said was true. A wife belonged to her husband. She had no rights, save those he granted her, which could be withdrawn at any time.

Why had she not thought of all this before? When she had envisaged her plan, Lord Mountwood had been as

40

insubstantial as a phantom. Now she found herself confronted by reality and she knew that she simply must escape.

It was just a question of being firm.

"You are mistaken, my Lord," she said emphatically.

"There's no need for you to call me 'my Lord'," he replied. "It's very flattering, of course, and implies a submissive attitude that is very proper in a wife. But since we are married I shall permit you to call me Ivan."

"Since we are *not* married I shall call you 'my Lord'. And even if we were married I should not be submissive."

"Oh, but you will be. I shall insist upon it."

"You will not get the chance."

"You think so, do you? I can see that this is going to be a battle royal between us, but I shall win, because I shall tolerate nothing else. And while we're on the subject I may as well make it clear here and now that in future you will not contradict me. That's what submissiveness means, by the way. I thought I had better explain that, since I have a feeling you didn't know."

Unwisely Venetia allowed her temper to get the better of her.

"Oh, I know what it means. I've seen women treating their foolish husbands like deities, never having any opinions of their own – "

"Excellent!" he said cheerfully. "You do understand, after all. I see we're going to get on famously together."

"We are not going to get on together in any way," she told him sharply. "Since I am not going to India with you."

"Indeed?"

"I shall leave when we reach Portsmouth. I am sure an annulment can be managed discreetly."

"But there isn't going to be an annulment," he said

calmly. "And you are coming to India with me."

Venetia's eyes glinted.

"And how do you intend to get me on board, my Lord?"

"Oh, I shall drag you by the hair if I have to," he said brightly. "Or toss you over my shoulder, like a sack of meal. I really don't mind which."

"And I thought you didn't want to be laughed at! Just think of the scandal that will cause."

He seemed to consider this seriously.

"Do you know," he said at last, "I think you're right. Dragging you by the hair is out of the question."

"Good, and so – "

"And so I shall have to employ other methods."

He spoke so calmly that she did not realise what he meant to do. Moving too quickly for her to react, he came to sit beside her, seized her in his arms and drew her hard against him, looking down into her face with an expression that she could not read.

She just managed to whisper a wild, *"No!"* before his mouth descended on hers, silencing her protest, although inwardly she continued to protest vehemently.

But she knew now that he cared nothing for her inner thoughts. Mentally she might refuse him, but as long as he held her body in his arms, her mouth beneath his, he had all the consent he wanted.

She was his property. He had said so. And now it was clear that he intended to treat her as such.

Her thoughts whirled furiously, but already she knew that the real threat came from her own senses, which insisted on responding to this terrible man, despite the outrage he was inflicting on her.

The feel of his lips on hers was a wicked delight,

teasing and inciting her to respond. She wanted to experience that touch, wanted it desperately and with increasing fervour, so that she could not stop herself from moving her mouth against his, even while she was bitterly ashamed of herself for doing so.

She must resist him, she *must!* But how could she resist him when her senses yearned towards him, aching for him to claim her more deeply.

He drew back to look down on her and with one finger he traced the outline of her mouth. She gasped with the intensity of the sensation, but still she tried to fight.

"Let – me – go – " she stammered.

He laid his fingertip on the base of her throat where a pulse was beating madly.

"No," he said simply. "You want me as much as I want you."

"No," she cried frantically.

"Your mouth tells me one thing, your body says another."

He laid his lips over the little beating pulse, causing her to draw her breath in sharply, and dig her fingers into him as she was swamped by physical delight. She hated him for making her feel it, and hated herself even more, but nothing made any difference. She was invaded by a pleasure that made a mockery of her mind's rejection.

His kisses were moving up the length of her neck, to her chin, her mouth, renewing his assault there, purposeful, threatening, inviting, until she was dizzy.

She felt faintness begin to overcome her and fought to stay alert, but he was too much for her. He overwhelmed her with his virility and his sensual mastery, until there was nothing in the world but him.

She felt the train come to a halt, doors were opening.

She heard the Earl say,

"My wife has fainted. I will carry her."

She felt herself lifted up into his arms and was vaguely aware that he was descending from the train, walking a few steps, then climbing into a carriage.

This was the time to save herself, her last chance of escape. But her limbs were heavy, and her whole body was full of a terrible lassitude, as though she had been drugged.

And in a sense she had, but the drug was her own sensuality, unsuspected until now. But this fearsome man had detected it at once and used it unscrupulously against her, overcoming her independent will that she had thought so strong.

"To the ship, quickly," she heard him say. "My wife needs to rest as soon as possible."

The carriage was moving. She could already sense the salt air and hear the cry of the seagulls. In a few minutes they would reach the ship and it would be too late.

At last they rumbled to a halt. He was getting out and drawing her after him, lifting her high against his chest.

"Let me go," she whispered in despair.

"Never," he replied simply, and began to mount the gangway.

As they climbed higher and higher, she looked back over his shoulder at the ground falling away from them. It was too late. There was no escape now.

She heard the Earl say,

"Her Ladyship is unwell. Kindly show me at once to her cabin and set sail without delay."

As he began to carry her down some stairs and along a corridor, she could hear the sound of the engines, all ready for their departure.

At last the Captain threw open a pair of double doors.

"This is the Royal Suite, my Lord," he said. "I do hope her Ladyship will be better soon."

"I'm sure she will," the Earl said, carrying Venetia inside and laying her on the bed. "The excitement of our wedding day has overcome her. Please leave us now."

Only when the Captain had left did the Earl release her.

"Alone at last with my bride," he said in a mocking voice.

"How – dare – you!"

"Why should I not dare? We have the whole world before us and time to enjoy the delights of each other's company. In a few minutes the ship will depart and our honeymoon will have begun."

CHAPTER FOUR

"Will you please keep your distance from me?" Venetia said in a biting voice.

He shrugged and rose from the bed, but placed himself between her and the door.

"Don't try anything," he said.

All around her she could feel the ship vibrating as the engines hummed and the propellers whirred. Suddenly there was a small lurch and they were moving.

Venetia pulled off the bridal veil and ran to the porthole, through which she could see the quay beginning to glide past. They were on their way to India.

She turned a stony face on her abductor and found him regarding her sardonically.

"So now I'm your prisoner," she said.

"No, you're my wife."

"Is there a difference?"

"We can enjoy ourselves debating that another time."

"How can you possibly want to be married to a woman who hates you?"

He shrugged.

"Madam, I have as much concern for your feelings as you had for mine when you planned this escapade. Does that answer your question?"

She could think of nothing to say. He was right.

"Now," he said at last, "I think it's time for us to behave like newlyweds."

"If you imagine – "

"I mean that it's time we had a cosy, intimate dinner," he said smoothly. "I'm hungry, and I am sure you are too."

"I – dinner?"

"Of course, what were you expecting?"

"Nothing – I'm hungry," she admitted.

"Good, I suggest we change our clothes and then have dinner served. Luckily my valet went ahead to join the ship when I left the hotel this morning, so he is waiting for me in my dressing room. But you, of course, don't have your maid."

"I couldn't risk anyone coming with me who didn't have to."

"Very understandable. Can you manage alone?"

"Certainly," she replied stiffly.

"Good, then I shall leave you."

"There is still time for you to let me go," she said in a smouldering voice. "We can put in to shore – "

"I have no intention of doing any such thing. Understand that, once and for all."

He headed to his dressing room, but at the door he stopped and looked back.

"You have challenged me, madam, and I shall teach you what a mistake that was. I think we are both going to find the future very interesting."

He was gone before she could reply.

Furiously she began to open her bags, realising the problem she had given herself by coming without a maid. It couldn't be helped and she was better than most ladies at fending for herself. But she could have done with some assistance now.

Looking round her, she had to admit that the Royal Suite was extremely impressive, being luxuriously decorated and furnished.

There was an attractive sitting room with a desk, a table and some chairs. The walls were decorated with pictures which looked as though they had come from the Royal collection.

The suite even had two bathrooms, one for her and a separate one attached to the Earl's dressing room, which led off from the main bedroom.

She looked into the dressing room and saw one narrow bed. Then she looked at the large double bed in her own room.

It was a bed for honeymooners. And that was exactly what she was, as he had reminded her.

He came back into her mind, tall, broad-shouldered, handsome, and above all intensely virile. He was a man made to be loved by women. He would attract them wherever he went and they would lure him, because he knew he could have any one of them he wanted.

Inexperienced as she was, Venetia knew all this by instinct. No woman could possibly mistake the lusty gleam in his eye that said women were there to be enjoyed, and he would enjoy them at his leisure.

She guessed he was a man who had never been rebuffed or made an object of scorn by a woman. Hence his rage with her.

She knew that if they had met differently she too might have succumbed to the promise of unknown pleasure implicit in his every line. She could have fallen in love with his air of being master of the world.

But they had met as foes and now she must beware of the very things that drew her towards him. She could not afford to weaken, to soften or to yield an inch.

Not an inch.

For some reason the thought made her eyes fall on the luxurious engagement ring. It was a truly magnificent creation, with one large diamond surrounded by many small ones. He had given it to his future wife, but he had not meant it for her.

Slowly and deliberately she removed it from her finger and put it in the drawer of the dressing table.

When she had unpacked, she went into the bathroom and ran some water. As she lay down in the bath with the cool water flooding over her naked body, she thought of Mary, and hoped that all had gone well with her and she was married to David by now.

It was peaceful in this quiet little room and she needed time to think, but she could not stay here forever. Sooner or later she must rise and go forth to do combat with her enemy.

The armour she chose for the battle was the blue satin that she had worn on the first evening. It might not be an ideal choice, but the others were badly creased. This one had been packed at the last minute, and survived better.

She managed to put the dress on but at the last moment she encountered a problem. Without a maid there was no way she could do up the back.

"Oh no!" she cried furiously, turning this way and that in a vain attempt to reach the hooks and eyes.

There was a knock on her door.

"Is anything wrong?"

"No, everything's – I mean, it's all right," she called back hurriedly.

"It didn't sound like it."

"I just – have a small problem," she said through gritted teeth.

She was still struggling with her back to him as he said, "allow me to help."

Whirling, she saw that the Earl had come into the room and was standing there, watching her.

"How dare you come in here while I'm – ?"

"In a state of undress? It's as well that I did, or you could have remained that way for a long time. Luckily it's part of a husband's prerogative to act as lady's maid. Keep still while I do you up."

Her cheeks flaming, she had no choice but to stand still while he connected the hooks and eyes with an expertise that made her wonder how often he had done this before. Many times, if what she had heard was true.

When he had finished he stood back and surveyed her critically.

"Charming," he said, "although a little old-fashioned. You didn't buy that dress this year."

"No," she said defiantly.

"As Lady Mountwood you'll need to keep in the fashion. Never mind. The colour is admirable with your eyes. What jewels will you wear with it?"

"I was just about to go through my jewel case."

It was on the dressing table. He began to study it, seemingly not impressed.

"This will do for the moment," he said, holding up a small diamond necklace. "But you will need more jewellery as soon as it can be arranged."

His lofty tone stung her to say,

"I am quite content with what I have, thank you."

"But I am not and that is what matters."

He fell silent suddenly and she saw that he was looking

at her left hand, which now showed the wedding ring but not the engagement ring.

When he finally spoke his voice was deceptively light.

"Did you toss it overboard?"

"No, of course not. It's here."

She opened the drawer and showed him.

"I think you should take it," she said, holding it out to him. "I cannot wear it."

"And it's better to keep it safe," he agreed, taking it from her. "Now, stand still while I put this around your neck."

She was startled. She had not expected him to take her rejection of his ring so calmly. But he behaved as though the matter was closed.

She did as he said, standing quietly while he secured the necklace, feeling the soft brush of his fingers against her skin. She tried not to react, but she could not help the tremors that went through her at that whispering touch. It took all her self control not to shiver with physical delight, but she would die before she let him know how he affected her.

Except that he probably knew already? He was an experienced seducer, wise in the ways of women, with a hundred erotic skills at his command.

Not an inch, she reminded herself.

"Good," he said at last. "That will do until I can buy you something more suitable to your station in life. Now, I believe they are ready to serve dinner, so it's time for us to go."

He offered her his arm, she took it graciously, and together they walked into the room next door, where the table lay prepared. The cook was there and a waiter ready to serve them, both smiling at the newly married couple.

"I've prepared a special meal for the first evening of your marriage," the cook said. "I do hope the bride and groom with enjoy it."

"Thank you," the Earl said at once. "We are both of us very grateful and looking forward to it. Aren't we, my love?"

"Yes, indeed," she said.

They pulled out the chairs and the new husband and wife seated themselves on opposite sides of the small table.

To begin with everything was formality. The first course was served and the wine opened. They spoke to each other in measured tones, conscious of the presence of the waiter.

Venetia discovered to her surprise that she was extremely hungry. She had eaten little before leaving for the church and nothing since then.

At last the Earl signalled for the waiter to leave them.

"So now," he said when they were alone, "we can discuss matters calmly. I'm still rather vague about exactly how you managed all this. Those letters – "

"I wrote them. Mary's father has some stationery that he brought home from Windsor Castle. I wrote one letter to you, one to Sir Edward and one to the Captain of this ship."

"All from the Queen?"

"Of course."

"My congratulations. An excellent piece of organisation. And you fooled us all. You should have gone into the diplomatic corps."

"If they are ever enlightened enough to appoint women, I shall certainly do so," she said with spirit.

"You constructed an elaborate jigsaw puzzle, and all the pieces fitted perfectly. But for the merest chance, I wouldn't have known there'd been a substitution until we were at sea."

"That was the most important thing," she said. "You might have stopped the marriage and there would have been a tremendous uproar."

He stared at her.

"I think uproar would have been the least of it," he said at last.

"Well, arranging the marriage like that was crazy," Venetia said indignantly. "I thought that when I first heard about it. Then, when I realised how terrifying it was for Mary, I felt I had to do something to save her."

"And what about you? Did you never worry about your own fate?" he asked curiously.

"It was a tremendous effort on my part," Venetia told him, "to marry anyone in such an extraordinary way. But my father and mother are dead and I am my own mistress."

"Insofar as any woman is ever her own mistress," he observed dryly."

"Many woman are."

"The point is that they should *not* be. Independence is unnatural for a woman. She needs male guidance to prevent her making foolish use of her freedom."

"Well, I could hardly have done anything more foolish than marry you, could I?" she demanded tartly.

"Precisely. I'm glad you realise it. So, your parents are dead. Who were they?"

"My father was James Baydon, son of Sir Elroy Baydon, which I know you will find disappointing."

"Will I?"

"I am the granddaughter of a mere Baronet. Far too lowly for you."

"I shall endeavour to control my disappointment. What about your mother?"

"Her father was Viscount Daviton."

"So you are not entirely without titled connections? Good. Then I shan't need to throw you overboard."

He spoke so coolly that she could not be quite sure whether he was joking. Then she caught the gleam in his eye. It was a cold, cynical gleam, but there was humour behind it as well. She met it defiantly.

"I'm surprised you would bother to throw me," she said lightly. "I would think that as a dutiful, obedient wife I'd be expected to jump."

For a moment he was startled, then he raised his glass to her in ironic salute, observing,

"It had not occurred to me that you intended to be dutiful and obedient. What a delightful surprise!"

"Do not rejoice too soon," she advised him. "I never said that was what I meant to be – only that you would expect it."

"After the trick you've played on me, I think it's the least I can expect. You seem to have thought of everything," the Earl said in a somewhat sarcastic voice, "except me and my feelings."

"It is difficult to worry about you," Venetia told him, "you have everything. A great title, the favour of the Queen and the newspapers invariably describe you as the handsome Earl of Mountwood."

He gave a dismissive shrug.

"Newspapers!"

"I do agree," Venetia said earnestly. "They exaggerate so much, do they not? But, allowing you to be no more than passable looking, you still have all the advantages on your side."

"Except the privilege of choosing my own bride."

"That, from a man who allowed the Queen to choose his bride for him, is a thoroughly absurd objection. I would not have thought any man could agree to such an idea – even from the Queen – without making objections. It argues a meekness of character that fills me with dismay."

She had the pleasure of seeing that she had robbed him of speech. At last he managed to say,

"You will not find me meek, I assure you madam."

"I'm delighted to hear it. I should hate it if you were one of those men who is magnificent outside and a rabbit inside."

"Are you trying to provoke me?" he demanded with a flash of anger.

That flash told her that, despite his civilised air, he was still suppressing a deep rage that insisted on breaking to the surface now and then.

A wise woman would have tried to appease him. But perhaps Venetia was not very wise, for she said,

"If you were thinking clearly, you'd realise that you ought to be grateful to me."

"Grateful! Upon my word, madam, you have a strange way of looking at things. Grateful to you for making a fool of me?"

"Grateful to me for *saving* you from looking a fool," she retorted. "How would you have felt if you had arrived at Mary's home that night to discover that she'd already fled? Or worse, if you'd turned up at the church and had a long, and extremely public wait at the altar, only to discover that the bride was not coming?"

She could see by the chagrin in his face that this had hit home.

"What would you have done then?" she demanded. "Or can I guess? You'd have forced her, wouldn't you? You'd probably have dragged her to the altar by her hair, since that is your self-proclaimed method of dealing with any woman who doesn't bow down before your mightiness."

"Don't be ridiculous!" he growled. "I would have done nothing of the sort."

"Oh really? That treatment was to be saved for me, was it?"

"I mean I wouldn't have forced her to marry me."

"You wouldn't have had to. Her parents would have done the forcing if I hadn't stepped in. I told you before, Mary is carrying another man's child. Perhaps a son. How would you have liked to discover that after the wedding?"

He glared at her. "I wouldn't," he snapped.

Then he sat in bitter, brooding silence and she thought she had never seen a man's face so harsh and forbidding.

"Then maybe what I did wasn't so very terrible, after all," she suggested.

"You'll be wanting me to thank you next," he growled.

"You don't have to thank me," Venetia said. "What I did, I did for Mary. I want her to be very happy with the man she loves. In fact, I think that it's the only way to be happy."

"Then what about your own happiness?" he asked. "Married to a man you don't love?"

After a moment's thought she decided to tease him.

"When a woman becomes an old maid of twenty-four, she has to stop being sentimental and settle for what she can get."

To her surprise he gave a cackle of laughter.

"So you decided to settle for me?"

"No, I decided to settle for adventure. The thing that influenced me most was the fact that you were going to India. If I can't have love, I'll have excitement, that's what I say."

"Do you indeed?"

"Women get so little excitement, you see. You couldn't

expect me to give up such a chance."

He stared at her. Young ladies who talked like this were quite outside his experience.

"I suppose," she said at last, "it's time I asked you why we're going to India and what we're going to do there."

"We shall land at Bombay, which is luckily a shorter voyage than it used to be. At one time we'd have had to sail around the horn of Africa, but now we can cross the Mediterranean to Egypt, then pass through the Suez Canal to the Red Sea."

"And at Bombay, what do we do?"

"We board the train for Calcutta, where we shall stay with the Viceroy for a few days."

"The Viceroy!" Venetia breathed.

The Viceroy of India was the representative of Queen Victoria, who had been proclaimed Empress of India two years earlier. The current Viceroy was Lord Lytton, who lived and ruled in great splendour at Raj Bhavan, his palace in Calcutta.

And she was going to stay there!

"I'm going chiefly because Her Majesty wants a report about what's happening on the North-West frontier," he went on.

"The North-West frontier!" she exclaimed, filled with delight. "How wonderful!"

He gave her an odd look.

"What do you know about the frontier?" he asked.

"Only what everyone knows. The trouble is with the Russians who are determined, sooner or later, to conquer India, and take it away from us."

"That is something they will never do while I am alive," the Earl answered firmly. "Her Majesty is determined to keep India as part of the Empire. As for 'everyone knowing', I'm not sure that everyone does. Certainly most ladies don't."

Venetia clasped her hands.

"But how could anyone not be inspired by the thought of the Great Game?" she asked ecstatically. "I've been reading about it for years and it's the most wonderful, thrilling adventure."

"And just what do you imagine the Great Game to be?" he asked sardonically.

"It's a battle between England and the Russians, who want to expand into the countries between India and Russia – Afghanistan, Turkestan, Tibet, Mongolia, right up to the border with India and maybe right into India. We have troops on the frontier, but also explorers and archaeologists who are really spies, sending back news all the time."

"And just because one misguided romantic described it as a 'Great Game', you think it's fun?"

"Well, it's got to be more interesting than sitting home sewing," she said tartly.

He grinned.

"Besides," she added, "it's hardly fair to call Captain Connolly a misguided romantic, when he died for his beliefs."

He stared at her, a glimmer of respect dawning in his eyes.

"Captain Connolly," he echoed. "You really do know about it, don't you? There isn't one woman in a million who would know that name."

"Papa once met a man who had actually known him," she said in a tone that was almost reverent.

Captain Arthur Connolly had been one of the 'explorers' whom she had mentioned, until he had been captured by the Emir of Bukhara, a city in Turkestan. The

Emir had accused him of spying for the British Empire, which was probably true, forced him to dig his own grave and then had him ceremonially beheaded.

That had been nearly forty years ago, but his name lived on, especially in military and diplomatic circles, because he had coined the phrase 'the Great Game' and played the game to the end.

"And we're going to play the Great Game," she breathed.

"*We* most certainly are not," he said at once, sounding aghast. "I will be on a tour of inspection. You will sit sedately in the Viceregal mansion in Calcutta, waiting for me to return."

She made a face. "Not sedately."

"No, I don't suppose you've ever done anything sedately in your life."

"Anyway, it's dangerous," she countered. "Suppose you don't return?"

"Then you will be a rich widow and everyone will say how fortunate you are," he responded tartly.

She smiled at him, refusing to answer his riposte.

"I think," he said slowly, "that neither of us is exactly what the other expected. I didn't even know that women like you existed."

"Then your experience of women has been sadly limited," she told him.

"Nonsense," he said at once. "My experience of women has been – "

He checked himself, seeing, too late, the trap she had laid for him and the blind way he had walked into it.

Venetia saw him looking at her and there was something in his eyes that was almost respect.

CHAPTER FIVE

The waiter returned with champagne and they toasted each other courteously.

A silence fell. Venetia became aware that her new husband was looking at her intently. It was growing late and suddenly she could not meet his eyes.

"Well, madam?" he said.

"Do you think we could take a turn around the deck?" she asked. "I should like to look at the sea."

"You're right," he said. "I believe we are expected to show ourselves, looking and behaving like a newly-married couple."

Offering her his arm, he led her out of the suite and up to the main deck. As he had predicted the sight of them aroused much interest.

The night was velvety black around them, the darkness broken only by the lights from the ship, the stars and the full moon.

If she had married for love, she thought, this would have been the perfect, romantic wedding night. Wherever she looked she saw the crew, keeping a polite distance and smiling as if to say that all the world loves a lover.

But they were not lovers and she felt that she must find something neutral to talk about.

"It is certainly a magnificent ship," she said at last.

"Could it be anything else," the Earl asked, "when it was designed for Her Majesty? She has only used it once or twice, but it's still a Royal ship and few people get to use it."

"Then I feel very honoured. I was only hoping we wouldn't have one of those over-crowded and dirty vessels which usually are en route to the East."

"So you have travelled quite a lot?" he enquired.

"Yes, but not like this."

The Earl gave her a wry look.

"You're talking as though this was an adventure," he said, "instead of a bout of hostilities."

"Why shouldn't it be both?" she asked lightly. "There's nothing like a little hostility to add spice to life."

"Good grief! I think you mean that."

"I do. One always has to fight for anything which is worth having. Any history book will tell you that."

"And what did you decide to fight for?"

She thought before answering this.

"For a life that was different," she said at last. "One where every day isn't exactly like the day before."

"So you ventured out into the unknown? Have you no sense of danger at all?" he demanded.

"If I had, I should not admit it to you. Or even to myself. That would be fatal."

"Which would be the more fatal?" he asked at once. "To admit it to me, or to yourself?"

She considered.

"I haven't decided that yet."

"When will you decide?"

"Perhaps I never will."

"There's no doubt that your mind works differently to

any woman I have ever met. What has made you so different?"

Venetia thought for a moment. Then she said,

"I've been alone since my parents died, and I've had to think for myself and plan for myself. At last I decided that, whatever happens, I must meet life unafraid and be ready for anything."

"You've certainly done that. I like the fact that you have a brain, unlike so many women, and I like the way you use it. It might even be useful to us both in whatever lies ahead. Perhaps not entirely for ourselves, but for the country we are representing."

"I do hope so," Venetia agreed. "The trouble with most people is that they feel rather than think. So often, because they don't use their brains, they lose the battle."

"What a very combative person you are! Do you realise that you discuss almost everything in terms of battle?"

"No, I hadn't realised that," she mused. "But it's true."

As she spoke the ship gave a sudden lurch. At once his arms were about her, holding her steady.

"We've reached the Bay of Biscay," he said, "and it's usually a bit choppy, but don't be afraid."

To his astonishment she turned shining eyes onto him.

"I'm not afraid," she said. "I always love this part of the trip."

"So you have been this way before?"

"Many times. My parents both loved travelling and I think I was only three when I was first taken on board a ship. After that I sailed more or less every year."

"That means you are not afraid of being seasick," the Earl remarked, "and you won't beg me, as women have begged me before, to make the ship go slower so that they would not be thrown about."

"I rather like the sea when it's rough," Venetia said. "I have been in the Bay of Biscay so often that it almost isn't exciting any more."

"I'm sorry for that, madam," he said ironically. "I naturally hope to provide you with as much excitement as possible."

"Never mind. I shall have all I want when we reach India. That's a country I long to see."

"Yes, I gather from what you said earlier that if I'd been stuck in the country you wouldn't have looked at me."

"Well, I'm used to a quiet country life," she pointed out. "There would have been no novelty. Let's talk some more about India."

"I think not," he said. "Some of your ideas make me nervous."

At that moment another great wave made the ship lurch, so that once more they were forced to cling together.

"It's going to be very rough," he said.

"Good," she said firmly. "The rougher the better."

"But perhaps we should go below."

"You go if you want to. I'm enjoying myself."

He could see that this was true. She was instinctively swaying with the ship, so that she kept her balance without trouble.

Now the wind was gathering force, making the sea heave and the boat rear up. The Earl felt spray lash his face and looked at Venetia to see if she was troubled. But it was clear that she was enjoying herself. He had a glimpse of her face with its shining eyes and look of blissful expectancy.

Then she turned away and went to stand by the railing, bracing herself against it and staring out over the sea. She had arranged her fair hair as best she could, unaided, but several curly strands had come loose and fell over her face and down about her long neck.

Now the wind was blowing these back, giving her the appearance of an old-fashioned ship's prow. She looked wild and magnificent, standing there, confronting the gale, defiant and unafraid.

He began to wonder just what kind of woman fate had caused him to marry unknowingly. So far she had been full of surprises and he had a feeling that there were many more to come. He could not say whether the prospect filled him with pleasure or unease. At this moment it was about equal.

The air was growing chilly and he thought he saw her shiver.

"You should have worn a shawl out here," he said, regarding her daringly low-cut gown, revealing the soft swell of her bosom that just vanished into the material at the exact moment demanded by propriety.

All evening he had feasted his eyes on that sight in the soft light of their suite. Even now he could see the smooth perfection of her skin, no longer glowing and golden, but turned to white marble in the moonlight.

He had no objection to her offering her beauty to his eyes like this, but he had every objection to the other men on the ship being afforded such a treat.

"You must cover yourself," he insisted, adding hastily, "or you'll take a chill."

"I don't need anything," she said, not taking her eyes from the sea where the foam gleamed white.

She put her head back, so that her face was lifted to the moon and took a deep breath, as though wanting to drink in every moment of the experience.

Without wasting further words he hurriedly removed his coat and wrapped it around her, placing his hands on her shoulders to prevent the coat falling off.

He thought he sensed a tremor go through her, but he could not be certain. And she gave no other sign of acknowledging his presence.

The ship's Captain approached them.

"May I suggest, my Lord, that you should both go below? We've entered the Bay of Biscay and it's going to be a rough crossing."

"But I love rough crossings," Venetia insisted.

"The Captain's word is law, my love," the Earl said. "He wants to concentrate on negotiating the Bay without having to worry about us."

As he spoke he tightened his grip, so that she had no choice but to turn and walk with him towards the steps that led down to their suite.

Once there he took her straight to her room. She heard the click as he locked the outer door so that nobody could disturb them.

Then he slipped the coat from her shoulders.

"I'll help you undress," he said softly.

"What?"

She whirled, looking at him, alarmed. "There's no need – "

"Can you undo this dress alone?"

"No," she admitted reluctantly.

He turned her round and began to work on the hooks and eyes. She felt his hands moving lower until they reached her waist and waited for him to release her. Instead he dropped his head and laid his lips against her bare shoulders.

Venetia tensed, her heart thumping wildly. There was something about the gentle touch of his lips that sent wild tremors flickering through her. She had meant to be sensible, to find a way to fend him off until she was ready. That was the common sense thing to do.

But her body knew nothing of common sense. It only knew what it wanted and it wanted this man's touch.

As she hesitated he let his mouth drift in closer to her neck. He drew her back against him, turned her and held her hard against his chest.

Now she could sense that his heart was pounding as hard as her own. He was full of tension, determined to claim what he considered his by right. That was clear in every confident movement he made.

Too confident!

Something shouted in her mind that she must not allow this to happen. He thought he could take her for granted, and if she allowed him to do so, then she had lost the battle for ever. In his eyes she would be just another woman, to be treated no better than any other.

And with that thought came the strength for which she had prayed.

"No!"

Summoning all her strength she managed to release herself and step back.

"It's too soon for this," she said desperately.

"Too soon for me to make love to my wife, on our wedding night?"

"You know what I mean. I need more time."

"But surely you took all this into account when you forced yourself on me?" he asked sardonically.

He knew, of course, that she had taken none of it into account. She had thought of him in the abstract, but the reality of the real man was overwhelming. Her defences were almost shattered, leaving her with only a thread of self-respect to cling to.

But she would cling to that thread no matter what.

"Please let me go at once," she protested firmly.

He paused, leaning back to look at her.

"I must admire your courage, madam. You have no way of preventing me."

"No way? Suppose I appeal to your sense of honour?"

"What honour would I violate by making love to my wife?"

"Your sense of decency then," she flashed.

"You belong to me – "

"You are mistaken. I might, one day, belong to you. But not if you force me now."

They held each other's gaze, hers defiant, his fierce with desire.

His grip tightened, pulling her hard against him, lowering his head until his lips almost brushed hers.

"You dare to make terms with me?" he breathed, fanning her face with his hot breath.

She could not move, so tight was his grip on her arms. Then his hand was behind her head, holding it steady while his mouth covered hers in a kiss that was full of rage. There was no escape. She could only stand there while he assaulted her with his lips, silently demanding that she desire him and welcome him into her bed.

And she could have done so if things had been different. She knew that. But he was still a foe and if he insisted on his rights now, they would be enemies all their days.

The world began to swim. Her senses were hot and confused. Her strength was running out.

And then she felt him stop, as though turned to iron. A violent shudder went through him, and the next moment she felt herself lifted high in his arms and carried to the bed.

She had lost the battle she thought wildly. He meant to take her, whether she willed it or not. She could have wept.

Then she felt herself flying through the air as he tossed her unceremoniously onto the bed. She stared up at him, then realised, to her astonishment, that he was walking away to the door that led to his room.

As he pulled it open he swung round to face her, his face black with fury. His hand groped for the key, found it, tossed it onto the bed, where it landed just in front of her.

"Use it, madam," he said through gritted teeth. "Lock this door against me or by the devil himself, I won't answer for the consequences!"

Then he was gone, slamming the door behind him.

It took her a moment to realise what had happened, but at last movement returned to her limbs and she scrambled off the bed to run to the door.

She turned the key in the lock, knowing by instinct that he was standing on the other side, listening for that sound.

Then she slid to the floor sobbing, but muffling the sound, lest he hear that too.

*

In the early hours she awoke to find that the ship was still tossing. There was some light outside and she got out of bed, meaning to go to the porthole. But as she did so, a sudden plunge made her lose her balance, hitting her cheek against the wall of the cabin.

Rubbing her face, she made her way unsteadily back to bed and did not leave it again until the swell subsided. She drifted off to sleep again and was awoken by bright sunlight with the ship moving very slowly.

She washed quickly and dressed, choosing a skirt and blouse, so that there would be no need for the Earl to hook her up at the back.

She stared at the door to his dressing room, wondering if he would knock and try to join her, being unwilling to wait.

At last she left the suite and went up on deck, where a steward greeted her.

"Good morning, my Lady – oh!"

He looked shocked at the sight of her face and she rubbed the bruise self-consciously.

"Yes, I fell," she said. "That'll teach me not to walk about on a pitching ship. I would like to have breakfast on deck, if possible."

"Of course, my Lady. I'll set the table up beneath the awning over there."

She thanked him and went to sit under the awning, looking out over the sea and wondering why she could not yet see land. Her previous journeys had taught her that they should be nearing Gibraltar by now.

She was looking out over the rail when she became aware of the Earl by her side.

"You might have waited for me, my dear," he said in a voice of gentle reproach.

"Yes, I should have done," she said, conscious that they could be overheard. "But I was so anxious to see the water and the sun. I feel sure we must reach Gibraltar soon."

The Captain had appeared behind them.

"We should have done so by now, my Lady – " he began, but then he checked at the sight of her bruise.

It was on the far side to the Earl and he now saw it for the first time. She saw him get ready to ask about it, but then stop himself.

Of course, she thought. If he asked her, it would reveal that they had not spent the night together. She owed it to him to protect his dignity.

"Yes, it's beginning to look very ugly, isn't it?" she said

to him. "Good morning Captain. I've already told the steward how I fell against the wall. My husband warned me not to walk about while the ship was still lurching, but I wouldn't listen."

Beside her she sensed the Earl relax.

"Wives never do, unfortunately," he said.

"That's true, my Lord. My own wife never heeds a word I say. Breakfast will be served on deck as you wished, my Lady. The table is almost ready."

"You think of everything," the Earl said, leading her to the breakfast table and holding the chair for her until she was seated. "But I'm concerned about that bruise. It looks painful."

"Nothing I didn't deserve," she said lightly. "You warned me just before it happened, remember?"

He met her eyes.

"Thank you for that," he said quietly.

"It is I who should thank you," she said, also quietly. "I appreciate what you did last night."

Before he could answer the Captain appeared again, asking if everything was to their satisfaction.

"Very much so," the Earl said cordially. "But we seem to be travelling rather slowly, which puzzles me."

"I'm afraid the ship sustained some damage in the storm last night," the Captain said. "I believe one of the propellers may be damaged, but I can't be certain until we reach Gibraltar. And I'm afraid that we have to limp there."

The Earl made a wry face.

"That's regrettable, but it can't be helped," he said. "Let's just hope it doesn't delay us for too long."

When they were alone he said,

"A small delay in Gibraltar may even be useful. We can increase your wardrobe. Of course, Lady Mountwood's clothes should really be individually made by seamstresses, but we'll have to manage without that."

"Clothes," she said, trying not to sound too pleased.

"Up-to-date clothes," he said, picking up her tone. "Although probably not actually fashionable."

"When I've been to Gibraltar in the past I've been surprised at how fashionable they manage to be," she said. "They get all the recent magazines, and copy them. In fact, I remember one shop that was especially good – "

"Excellent. We'll go there."

A sense of relief had fallen over them both. This small crisis would give them something to talk about while they circled warily about each other.

"Did you sleep well?" he asked politely.

"Very well, thank you."

"Your dreams weren't haunted by – remorse, shall we say?"

"It never crossed my mind," she assured him truthfully. "And you?"

"Are you suggesting that I should feel remorse? For what, may I ask?"

"For nothing," she conceded with a faint smile. "I suppose, if we're being fair, I should consider myself lucky that you didn't toss me overboard, instead of – "

She stopped, blushing slightly.

"Instead of simply onto the bed," he finished for her. "You'll never know how hard it was for me to walk away."

After a moment he added,

"Or perhaps, one day, you *will* know."

He spoke so softly that she was not quite sure she had heard him properly. Then she realised that he had left her free to acknowledge his words or pretend not to have heard them. And she was glad, for she would not have known what to say.

And yet her heart could not help echoing,

'One day – one day – '

With practical matters to be considered, they found that the time passed without awkwardness. They spent part of the day looking over the railing, watching the port of Gibraltar appear and grow very slowly nearer.

Over lunch his mood became a little tense, and Venetia realised that those of the crew who dared were regarding him with shock and even a slight hostility.

"You realise that this is your fault?" he growled. "It's that bruise on your face. They think I did it."

She gave a choke of laughter.

"It isn't funny."

"Of course it isn't," she said, straightening her face with an effort. "We have to convince everyone that you are a model husband, the perfect gentleman, full of refinement, gentle manners, courtesy – "

"You'll drive me too far, madam."

"Well it might help if you stopped calling me 'madam' in that formal way," she pointed out, still amused. "The husband of my dreams would call me Venetia, or even beloved."

"And precisely when did I become the husband of your dreams, *beloved?"*

"I thought I'd already told you that. When I discovered you were going to India."

After a sulphurous silence he gave her a reluctant grin.

"Well, you might do something to restore my reputation," he growled. "Otherwise, I shall never live this down."

"All right," she said, relenting.

The steward was approaching with coffee, and several other crew members were nearby.

Rising from her seat, she went to stand behind the Earl's chair, slipping her arms about his neck and leaning down to rest her cheek against his.

The waiter served the coffee, careful not to look at them too obviously, but there was no way he could have missed her gesture of affection.

"My dearest," she purred, turning her face slightly towards him.

At the same moment he turned to her and their eyes met, very close. His gleamed with interest, hers with challenge.

Then his hand moved swiftly, cupping her head so that his lips could brush hers.

"My darling," he murmured.

He kissed her again, more firmly this time, his hand still imprisoning her head.

Very well, she thought. This was a game that two could play.

She managed to place her hands on either side of his face while she gave him her own kiss, firm and purposeful, her lips moving over his again and again. To her great satisfaction she could feel his astonishment.

"You're playing a dangerous game," he whispered against her lips.

"I'm playing the game you want me to play," she whispered back.

At the same moment they released each other and drew back a little, eyes meeting eyes.

Each knew that their battle of wits had passed into a new phase. Each was glad of it, and knew that the other was also glad.

CHAPTER SIX

It was late when the *Angelina* edged very slowly into Gibraltar harbour. The sun had almost finished setting and they decided to go ashore to dine.

A steward was sent for a carriage and soon they were ready to step ashore and go exploring.

"Why don't we first go to that shop you mentioned?" the Earl said. "Then we can discover if it's still there and afterwards find a place to eat."

To her delight the dressmakers was exactly as she had last seen it.

"We'll return first thing tomorrow morning," he said.

"You don't think the Captain will want to leave tomorrow?" she asked anxiously.

"I don't think he can start the repairs before morning. We'll be here a couple of days, so we may as well enjoy it."

They let the carriage go and strolled along Main Street looking into shop windows. Some of them were still open and they managed to buy a copy of *The Times* that had just arrived from England.

"But it's much too soon for anything about the wedding to appear in a newspaper," he said, in a voice that asked for reassurance.

"Of course," she agreed. "But it will. I wonder what

they'll say, or whether they will realise what has happened."

"I devoutly hope not," he said. "I need time to arrange that story before our return to England."

They were passing a very large and luxurious restaurant. He led the way inside and soon they were settled at the best table.

The Earl took great care ordering the meal, consulting her taste and inviting her opinion, deferring to the fact that she had been here before, and he had not. But he did not consult her before saying,

"And the best champagne you have in the cellars."

When the bottle arrived and they each held a glass, Venetia returned to the subject.

"Don't you mean that *we* need time to arrange our story?" she enquired sweetly.

"Yes, I'm sure that's what I meant," he said with resignation. "I dare say you are already making schemes inside that devious head if yours."

"Well, they'd love the truth," she mused. "All about how you were deceived into marrying someone you'd only met once before, and then discovered that you weren't even clever enough to make sure you had the right bride. Did you say something?"

The Earl had made a noise.

"Nothing," he growled.

"I thought you said something."

"I was actually suppressing my thoughts for fear of alarming you," he said. "But I forget that nothing alarms you."

"True. So you need not suppress anything that comes into your mind. Although I imagine I can guess these thoughts. Just think! All those headlines about the unwanted bride."

"I could hardly want you if I'd only met you the night before," the Earl pointed out.

"Which is also when you met the bride you did not want," Venetia said sharply.

The Earl laughed.

"I'd forgotten that for a moment. But it was crazy of me, Queen or no Queen, to think of marrying a girl who might have been hideous to look at and ghastly to talk to."

Venetia knew it was unwise to show any interest, but she couldn't resist saying,

"And?"

"You're interesting to talk to, I'll give you that."

She laughed aloud.

"Coward," she said. "You're lucky to have been palmed-off with no-one worse than me."

"Now you're fishing for compliments. I thought the moment I saw you, you were passably pretty."

"Passably?"

"I have extremely high standards," he replied apologetically.

"I've a good mind to throw this champagne over you."

"Don't do that," he said agreeably. "It's an excellent vintage and I believe they only have two more bottles.

As they were eating the first course he conceded,

"After our first conversation I realised you were also extremely intelligent. I'll even admit that I rather dreaded this voyage simply because there would only be one person to talk to. With most women I find their conversation ends in a day. After that they merely repeat themselves."

"Now you are being horrid and it is untrue," Venetia said. "Some women are very intelligent, like my mother. My father invariably asked her opinion on anything before he made up his mind.

"I didn't realise that until I was much older, and watched them together. They were very happy with each other and it is what I always hoped to find for myself."

"Only to be disappointed with me," the Earl said.

If he was hoping for a compliment he was deceiving himself.

"That isn't the right word," Venetia answered. "You were not *precisely* a disappointment – "

"Thank you ma'am," he said ironically. "I'm overwhelmed by the intensity of your enthusiasm."

"Well, you should not be. I assure you my enthusiasm for you is not at all overwhelming."

"I see," he said, chagrined.

"Although naturally I do my best," she added kindly.

He grinned suddenly.

"Little cat," he said, without anger.

Venetia chuckled.

"So," he went on, "if I am not *precisely* a disappointment, what – *precisely* – am I?"

"Well – " she said with a judicious air.

"Come along, be honest. Don't spare my feelings. Oh but how foolish of me. You weren't going to, of course."

"You really understand me very well after such a short time," she said.

"Yes, don't I? Right this minute I know you're planning to say something that will tease and infuriate me. And you'll say it with a smile."

"I think that's very unjust," she said with an air of injured innocence. "I was only going to say that you are different in every way from what I had expected."

"You didn't expect anything," he retorted at once. "You never gave the practicalities of the situation a moment's thought beforehand."

"That's true," she admitted with a sigh. "I suppose I never really thought of you as an individual at all. You were just like the little sugar groom that goes on top of the wedding cake."

"You move him here and move him there, but you don't expect him to have thoughts and feelings," the Earl supplied.

"Or the bride either. Any man who undertakes to marry a woman the day after meeting her, sees women as sugar dolls, which in fact is true of you. Your own words have confirmed it."

"*I?*"

"On the train to Portsmouth. I seem to recall we had a certain discussion about your ideal wife."

He cleared his throat.

"Never mind that. If I thought I was marrying a sugar doll, I have learned otherwise."

"So we were both surprised. Insofar as I had any expectations of you, they were that you would be very English and therefore limited in conversation, unless you were talking about hunting, shooting and fishing. At the same time, because you were a protégé of the Queen, I thought you would be very proud of yourself and somewhat of a snob."

"Did you really think I would be as bad as that?"

"It was not exactly bad," she replied, "but it is what one often finds in an Englishman while Frenchmen, Germans and Italians are quite different."

He considered this statement for a moment. Then he looked at her as though expecting her to say something. But the silence dragged on and on.

"Are you not going to ask me about my impressions of you?" he said at last.

Venetia looked at him out of bland, guileless eyes.

"No," she said simply. "Ah, here's the next course."

They fell silent while the waiter removed their plates, served more food and replenished the wine.

For a while they ate in silence, each waiting for the other to speak. The Earl was the one who gave in.

"All right, I'll tell you. When I saw you for the first time for dinner at your Uncle's house, I thought you were very pretty. In fact too pretty to be good at anything except being kissed and your conversation would be limited to the compliments you expected me to pay you."

"I only wish," Venetia said, "I had something I could throw at you. That was an insult."

"Really?"

"Why should you think I expected compliments when you were there to marry another woman? As you thought."

"As I thought," he echoed wryly. "My experience is that women always expect compliments, from any man, no matter what he's there for. If they don't get them, they're insulted. If they do get them, they're insulted on behalf of some other woman. A man never knows where he is or what is expected of him."

"Don't try to make yourself sound like an injured innocent," Venetia told him severely. "You will never be convincing."

"I bow to your greater wisdom in these matters, ma'am."

"And if it's a crime to look pretty and be willing to receive compliments, then in future I will dress myself in rags and treat a man as if he is dirt beneath my feet."

"You mean, like you treat me?" he demanded.

She smiled, but did not answer.

They did not linger over their coffee.

"We have a long and exhausting day buying clothes tomorrow," he said. "We should head back to the ship for an early night."

All the way back in the carriage, Venetia was wondering if the evening would end in the same way as last night.

As they stepped down to the suite he said,

"I ought to thank you for your generosity."

"How?"

"I'm talking about your bruise, and the way you made it clear to everyone that I was not to blame, and also concealed the fact that I slept in another room."

She faced him.

"I fight fair," she said.

He nodded.

"So I see. But tell me one thing. Am I really blameless?"

"I don't understand."

"When I threw you onto the bed – are you sure it didn't happen then? I turned away at once and didn't see whether, perhaps, I had injured you."

"You didn't," she assured him. "You are not to blame, in any way. What is it?"

She asked because he was regarding her with a look of quizzical irony.

"You missed your chance," he said.

"My chance to do what?"

"To put your foot on my neck. You had only to say that I was the brute who had injured you and I couldn't say anything. You had me at your mercy, and you let me go."

"But of course I did," she replied at once. "Why should I want a foe whose neck is beneath my heel? There's no fun in that."

"And what would you consider 'fun'?"

"A fair fight, face to face, man to man."

"By heaven, madam, you have a strange idea of fun! Let's fight man to woman. There's far more 'fun' in that."

"I shall look forward to it."

He raised her hand to his lips.

"The truth is as I said. You are a generous woman."

"Certainly not," she said, shocked. "I just enjoy drawing matters out."

"Do not argue with me, madam. I say you are generous and you have earned my respect. There isn't another woman alive who could have resisted such an opportunity to gain advantage over a man. What a rare being you must be."

While she struggled to find an answer, he turned her hand over and brushed his lips against her palm. At once she was swept by a tide of sensation that almost made her gasp.

It streamed along her arm, then right through her, inflaming her whole body with thrilling sensation.

The force of it almost overpowered her, but she fought back, refusing to let him know. Things were better between them, but she knew there was still a long way to go.

She looked up and for a moment their eyes met.

Then he released her hand.

"Goodnight," he said. "Sleep well."

And he walked away without another word.

*

The next morning they returned to the shop, where the owner recognised Venetia and at once plunged into the exciting job of providing her with a new wardrobe in double quick time.

She promised that every seamstress in Gibraltar would be pressed into service and several new gowns would be ready by that evening.

They spent the day sightseeing, visiting the rock and seeing the apes. Venetia discovered how pleasant it could be to travel with someone who enjoyed a good argument.

She had been too young when she was with her father to argue with him, even though she listened to him having serious and often important conversations with other men.

Looking back she thought they took themselves very seriously and seldom laughed.

It was quite different from the way she argued with the Earl, as they seemed to end up by laughing not only at each other but at themselves.

That evening they dined with the Captain and the First Officer. The Captain explained that there would be a further delay as he had sent for a new engine part. But he hoped it would arrive tomorrow and they could proceed the day after.

As he spoke he could not resist a glance of admiration at Venetia, who was looking ravishing in a new gown of primrose yellow tulle. He averted his gaze quickly, but the First Officer was less successful.

He was a young man whose experience of beautiful girls was limited and Venetia's presence overwhelmed him. Try as he might he could not prevent his eyes straying in her direction and staring at her, in defiance of propriety, until a cough from his Captain recalled him to reality.

The Earl watched, saying nothing, smiling enigmatically.

"That young man is in love with you," he said as they strolled on deck on the moonlight after dinner.

"Oh, nonsense!" she said lightly.

"Don't tell me nonsense. He's got the look of a dying

calf – a sure sign. I'm sure you've seen it often enough. Come Venetia, you must have seen enough men in love with you to be able to tell."

"I certainly thought he admired me," she said. "But perhaps he was just being polite."

"You don't believe that. And you haven't answered my question."

"Did you ask one?"

"I asked about the men who have been in love with you."

She shrugged.

"I've lived a very quiet life," she sighed. "It has not been full of male company, as you seem to suggest."

"Have *you* ever been in love?"

"I have met quite a number of men since I 'came out'," she said, "but I have not fallen in love. I thought I was in love once and became engaged. But he broke it off because I was not rich enough and I forgot him easily.

"There was another man my parents wanted me to marry, but I didn't love him at all. They were very upset, but I wanted love, the love which comes from the heart and the soul, and is very hard to find."

"And don't you still want that?" he asked, looking at her curiously.

"It's an ideal," she said with a sigh. "But life doesn't live up to the ideal, does it? Or not very often. Haven't you found that?"

"Yes," he said slowly. "Of course I have been attracted by women but, somehow, they have disappointed me and never made me feel I couldn't live without them."

"That is what Mary felt," Venetia said. "In fact she said she would rather die than not be married to the man she loves."

"Can we not discuss Mary any more?" he asked in a rather tense voice. "I think it's time to leave her behind and concentrate on ourselves."

"Yes, we should leave her far behind," Venetia agreed. "She has made her choice, and I believe she will be very happy."

"And what of you and I, who have no choice?" he asked.

"Perhaps we still do. It may yet be possible for us to part quietly."

"You think so, do you?" he asked quizzically.

In truth, she did not. There were feelings inside her now that she knew would make it impossible for her to leave him. But she did not want to look at them too closely as yet.

"I think I'll retire," she said hurriedly. "Goodnight."

"Goodnight, my dear."

He did not try to accompany her below, but stood by the rail watching until she had disappeared. Then he turned and stared out over the water.

*

Next day they returned to the shop where Venetia's new wardrobe was being assembled. The Earl paid out a sum that seemed enormous to her, but which he barely seemed to notice. Then, after a leisurely lunch, they made their way back to the ship.

It was as the carriage was drawing up on the quay that Venetia suddenly said,

"Look, over there."

"Where?" He was trying to follow her pointing finger.

"That man. It looks like Lord Anthony."

"It can't be. What could he be doing – good heavens!"

The tall willowy young man, at whom they were both

looking, turned and waved to them, his face brilliant with delight.

"By all that's wonderful, it is Anthony," the Earl cried. *"Here old fellow!"*

They both stepped down from the carriage as Lord Anthony began to run towards them.

"I say," he called eagerly. "I say."

The two men clasped each other in a vigorous bear hug, while Venetia stood watching them, smiling with pleasure at the sight of her husband's friend, for whom she had felt a great sympathy.

Suddenly he caught sight of her and his eyes nearly popped out of his head.

"I say!" he said. "It's Miss Baydon. But what are you – ?"

"It's a long story," the Earl said.

"But – Lady Mountwood – ? I mean – "

"Lady Mountwood has no objections," the Earl assured him, grinning. "Come aboard, old fellow, and tell us how you come to be here."

They had tea on deck under the awning. Lord Anthony could not take his eyes from Venetia and clearly there would have to be explanations, but before that they both wanted to know what had happened after they left.

"It was the strangest wedding reception I ever attended," their friend confessed. "No bride and no groom with everyone looking to me for an explanation."

"But why you?" Venetia asked.

"I was the best man. I was supposed to know everything," Anthony said simply.

This was too much for his sorely afflicted companions and they both burst into hearty laughter.

"I'm sorry," the Earl said at last, wiping his eyes. "It's

the thought of you knowing everything – "

"I didn't know anything," Anthony replied, aggrieved. "But they thought I should. Sir Edward said something about letters from the Queen making you leave quickly.

"But then nobody could think where Miss Baydon was. You had just vanished into thin air, ma'am. Then someone said you must have gone with the bride and groom. Well, I knew you hadn't, because I saw them off and you weren't with them."

"What happened when you told everyone that?" Venetia asked.

"Nothing. I didn't tell them. I just got out as fast as I could before the place became too hot to hold me."

"Very wise," the Earl said, his eyes twinkling.

"But I don't understand, Miss Baydon. How did you manage to catch up?"

"She didn't. She came with me," the Earl told him.

"But there were only two of you in the carriage."

"Meet my bride," the Earl said, indicating Venetia.

"But – when – ?"

"The substitution was made before we started for the church," added the Earl, adding wryly, "My 'bride' unaccountably preferred another man."

Lord Anthony drew a sharp breath. His eyes were wide with horror.

"And you forced Miss Baydon to marry you instead? I say Ivan, that's not – I mean – how could you?"

He ground his teeth.

"I did not force Miss Baydon to do anything. It was she who effectively forced *me* by substituting herself behind the veil. I had no idea until we were on the train. Don't waste your pity on her, Anthony. Save it for me."

But Lord Anthony's chivalrous instincts had been aroused.

"He slanders you ma'am, I'm certain of it. He dragged you on board by force."

"Actually, that's not far from the truth," Venetia mused with a wicked glance at the Earl, who glared back.

"Aha! I knew it. This is abduction. And you even wounded this poor lady."

"What?" they both asked together.

In a fury Anthony pointed to the bruise on Venetia's face.

"You *cad,* sir!" he exclaimed. "How could you do such a thing to a defenceless female?"

"Defenceless!" the Earl snorted.

"Madam, I stand ready to rescue you. Come with me at once and we will leave this ship of infamy. Accept my protection – "

"Oh, shut up, for pity's sake!" the Earl said in disgust. "It's like sitting through a bad performance at the theatre. Someone should throw rotten tomatoes at you."

"Sir, you may scoff but – *madam!"*

This last outraged protest was drawn from him by the fact that Venetia was crowing with laughter.

"I'm sorry," she said when she could speak, "but I truly don't need rescuing. The quieter we keep the story the better. None of us wants a scandal."

Anthony blenched. The prospect of scandal dampened his chivalrous fire and at last he allowed her to calm him down.

"I don't understand," he said for the tenth time.

"Well, I don't understand why you came to this spot when you made your escape," she said. "Were you trying to catch up with us?"

"Oh no. I never dreamed that you could still be here."

"We wouldn't be if a propeller hadn't broken," the Earl told him.

"Ah, so that's it. I came to Gibraltar because my uncle has a villa here and I thought I'd be safe. But now, I'm not so sure. My aunt is determined to find me a wife and as soon as she sees me she'll get to work. The prospect terrifies me."

"You mean they don't know you're here yet?" the Earl asked.

"That's right. I left my bags at the station while I tried to pluck up courage to go to their villa."

The Earl and Venetia exchanged smiling glances and both nodded.

"Come with us," she voluntered.

"With – you mean to India?"

"Yes, why not?" the Earl said, thumping him on the back.

"I won't try to marry you off," Venetia assured him.

"Promise?"

"Promise."

"Then I'll come."

A sailor was despatched to the station to collect Anthony's valet and his luggage. Everything arrived within the hour, by which time a suite had been arranged for the newcomers.

Soon after that another carriage drew up at the ship bearing clothes from the dress shop.

The Captain announced that the repairs were complete and they would soon be under way. That evening the three friends made merry over dinner on deck, while the *Angelina* headed deep into the Mediterranean at full steam on its way to India.

CHAPTER SEVEN

When they reached Egypt the *Angelina* entered the Suez Canal that connected the Mediterranean with the Red Sea and shortened the trip to India by several weeks. As they glided down the hundred mile canal the three of them stood at the front of the boat, while the wind streamed past them.

"This is the life," Anthony sighed. "What are you expecting to do when you reach India, Mountwood?"

"I've been wondering that myself," the Earl replied. "I have to report back to Her Majesty of course, but I think, from what I've heard, our troops need encouragement and reassurance that people at home have not forgotten them."

There was silence for a moment.

Then Venetia said,

"Of course, it's a very long way from England. If they have left behind their wives and children, it's miserable for them to be so far away from home."

"That is what all soldiers feel at one time or another," the Earl said. "I spent some time in the army myself and remember being rather lonely."

"Indeed?" Venetia teased. "I'm quite certain all the local girls were at your feet telling you how handsome and exciting you were."

"Oh, they were indeed," Anthony said eagerly. "They

all set their caps at him, ma'am, especially after they'd seen Mountwood Castle."

"Ah, it was the castle that attracted them not his manly charms," Venetia chuckled.

She and Anthony had become firm friends and by now he was in possession of the whole story. He had laughed heartily at the tale of how his friend had been deceived, and advised Venetia to make no rash decisions.

"Why shouldn't you leave him, if you want to ma'am?" he asked. "Serve him right."

"Excuse me, but I consider myself the aggrieved party in this matter," the Earl pointed out.

"A man always considers himself the aggrieved party," Venetia retorted. "I have by no means decided to remain with you. But even if we part I hope that, out of curiosity, I can visit your home, because I have heard so much about it." She sighed theatrically. "It might even make me regret leaving you – unless, of course, you turn me away at the front door."

The Earl laughed.

"I have a feeling if I did that you would somehow get in, even if it meant climbing down the chimney."

"Am I really as bad as that?" Venetia asked cheerfully.

"Not bad, but clever," he replied. "So far you have had your own way in everything. I think you'll achieve the same success a thousand times before you die."

In his turn, he too spoke theatrically, saying,

"But I must tell you, ma'am, that you are not at all the kind of woman I admire."

Lord Anthony looked from one to the other, shock registering on his face.

"You see," the Earl continued, "the trouble with you is that you are too perceptive. Women should be sweet and gentle, accepting what they are told without querying it or expecting something better."

"Nonsense!" Venetia exclaimed robustly.

"You see?" the Earl appealed to his friend. "She proves my point."

"You would be bored stiff," she told him, "with a woman who agreed with everything you said and thought it was heaven on earth just to have you with her."

"I see no reason why she should not feel like that," the Earl replied and his eyes were twinkling.

"Now you are being conceited," Venetia told him. "As I said at the beginning you are perfectly aware that women run after you and kneel at your feet merely because you are an Earl. If you were just plain Mister they wouldn't be half so persistent in their pursuit of you."

"That's perfectly true," Anthony told his friend earnestly. "Remember that girl who – ?"

"Yes, never mind," the Earl said hastily. "Well, dear wife, you've given me much to think about. I only hope I'll remember this conversation with you, when I find myself sitting alone in my smoking-room at home, and there is only the wind whistling outside the windows."

Now Venetia laughed.

"If you are sitting alone, it will be entirely your own fault," she told him. "As to remembering what I've said to you, you know if you're honest, that by the time you return home you'll be thanking Heaven that you no longer have this tiresome woman arguing with you."

"Oh, I say," said Anthony.

"I only hope," the Earl answered, "that by the time we return home, you will be paying me compliments."

Venetia knew, by the way his eyes were laughing, that he was only teasing her.

She merely replied,

"We'll have to wait and see. When you return you might be accompanied by a beautiful woman you've met in India, who'll be the wife you've always wanted."

"There's a flaw in your reasoning. I have never wanted a wife."

"Why that's true, of course. You wanted a wife so little that you obtained one by plucking her off the shelf at someone else's recommendation, and not even examining the goods properly before you registered them in your name."

The Earl roared with laughter and clapped Anthony on the shoulder.

"It's all right, old fellow. Don't let your eyes pop like that. We don't mean half what we say to each other."

"But which half is which?" Anthony said, unexpectedly putting his finger on the point.

Venetia and the Earl looked at each other, each wondering the same.

*

At last they reached the end of the Suez Canal and passed through the Red Sea, growing ever nearer to the Arabian Sea, and India.

One day, while the Earl was deep in discussion with the Captain, Anthony manoeuvred to get Venetia alone. She could see that something was troubling him.

"I say, I wish you'd forget those things I said the night before the wedding," he told her fervently.

"You mean about Ivan having the pride of the devil and liking to be master?" she enquired innocently.

"Well – I don't think I actually said – "

"Oh, but you did," she assured him, wide-eyed. "And you said he liked to be master and wouldn't want a wife who answered back or questioned his movements, or minded about his other women – "

"I never said that!" he almost squealed.

"Not precisely – "

"Not anything like it," he said, roused to unusual firmness by his terror at this conversation. "I never mentioned other women. You did."

"Yes, I did," she relented. "Although you more or less admitted it – "

"I – that is – well, you're safe enough on this ship, aren't you? I mean, there aren't any other women."

Venetia quelled the laughter that threatened to overwhelm her.

"Anthony, you should have gone into the diplomatic service," she said through quivering lips.

He brightened. "Really? I did think of it once, but Ivan said it was not a good idea."

"I wonder why. Never mind. Let's forget that whole conversation ever happened."

"Yes, let's."

He mopped his brow.

Lying in bed that night she thought about what they had said. A wise woman might have let herself be warned, but Venetia supposed she could not be very wise where the Earl was concerned. She had gone in the opposite direction, teasing, daring, contradicting him at every turn. It might sound dangerous, but instinct told her that it was the only way to win and keep his respect.

And respect was essential, she knew. Without it, no other feeling could survive and flourish.

*

The weather became unbearably hot as they moved through the Arabian Sea towards Bombay. Now they concentrated all their thoughts on what lay before them.

"How are you going to explain me?" Anthony asked, thinking of this problem somewhat belatedly.

"I shall say you are my aide-de-camp," the Earl announced grandly.

At last the moment came, and the ship glided into the port of Bombay. To Venetia's delight a band was playing on the quay and a guard of honour was waiting to welcome them to India.

She took a last glance at herself in the mirror, hoping that she looked her best and would be a credit to her husband and her country.

She then hurried to the Earl's side and they left the suite together.

"Now it starts," he said. "We are on our way to see the Viceroy, who is Her Majesty's official representative and don't forget that you are my wife."

"Whatever do you mean? What are you afraid I might do?"

"You might say something terrible with that sharp tongue of yours."

"I promise to consider every word twice."

"That might be worse!"

The guard of honour was led by a very impressive looking officer whose uniform proclaimed that he was a Colonel. As they watched, he came up the gangway to greet them.

He welcomed them and said he regretted the Viceroy could not come in person, but would be waiting for them in Calcutta.

While the two men were speaking, Venetia was looking round her. She was amazed at the colour she could see. There were Indians waiting with garlands of marigolds.

The brilliance of the saris seemed to be echoed in the

uniforms of the various soldiers of all ranks moving about the quayside.

There were vendors selling fruits of green, purple and orange. She could see some small children carrying coloured windmills and kites.

But above all there was the sunshine, golden and warm which covered everything with an orange haze.

At that moment a truck containing a great pile of baggage pushed past them amid cries from the porters to clear the way.

When their luggage had been brought ashore they said goodbye to the Captain of the *Angelina*, who said to Venetia,

"We will miss you very much, but then our loss is India's gain."

She thanked him for a very nice compliment and said how grateful to him she was for such an enjoyable journey. The Earl shook the Captain's hand and then the Earl and Countess of Mountwood proceeded down the gangway to receive their official greeting.

Whilst the exchange of courtesies was going on, Venetia looked around her at an enormous group of official buildings which stood like a massive palisade.

Some of the buildings had huge palm-mat awnings which shaded the windows and there were white-suited figures strolling high on the balconies while below them were crowds of Indians.

She could see stalls piled high with watermelons or vividly coloured glass bowls with drinks. There were men selling sweetmeats and tobacco, chapattis and fruit.

She could hear the people shouting and the creaking of wagon-wheels. Enormous loads were on the wagons drawn by bullocks.

Waiting for them was a large carriage. Gallantly the

Colonel handed her in, stood back to allow the Earl to precede him and they were on their way.

As they set off leaving a Corporal to see that all their luggage followed, Venetia found everything fascinating.

"We're going straight to the railway station," the Colonel told them, "where a special train is waiting to take you to Calcutta."

"I wish we could stay here a little while," Venetia said. "It's so exciting."

"I too wish you could stay," the Colonel answered gallantly.

Obviously from the way he looked at her and the way he spoke, he admired her.

She hoped the Earl was pleased that she was showing off so well.

She had the feeling of having stepped into a dream. The brilliant colours were unlike anything she had known before.

The dream-like feeling grew even greater, when they reached the station and were welcomed by a military band, playing the National Anthem. They stood up straight until it was finished and then the Colonel showed them aboard.

The train was a private one and as luxurious as the ship. It had been laid on especially for them and there were no other passengers. Instead, there was a luxurious saloon, furnished with armchairs and a kitchen just for them, their servants and their newly acquired aide-de-camp.

One carriage was taken up by a room with two narrow beds and a small bathroom just beyond. Venetia was a little taken aback by the discovery that she would have to share this room with the Earl. But there was no dressing room for him here.

Everywhere she looked she saw the Royal crest.

"It's a Royal train," she said.

"In effect, yes," the Earl told her. "The Queen – or the Empress of India as I should call her here – has never visited this country, but if she did, this is the train she would use. Until then, it belongs to the Viceroy, who represents her."

"It all looks splendidly comfortable," she observed.

"I hope it is. It's a thousand miles to Calcutta, and I hope we'll spend most of it asleep."

"How long will it take?"

"If we start soon we should reach Calcutta tomorrow afternoon. There we shall meet the Viceroy."

"Lord Lytton?" Venetia said.

He gave her a quick look of surprise.

"You know his name? I suppose you looked it up when you were planning this escapade?"

"No, I didn't have time for that. I already knew. I've always read the newspapers from cover to cover."

"I would have been surprised to learn that you hadn't," he said with a grin.

"It's not just newspapers, but novels. I've always been mad about them, and I must have read everything the novelist Bulwer-Lytton wrote. So when his son became Viceroy of India it caught my eye."

"So you'll win the Viceroy's heart by telling him you like his father's novels?"

"I might," Venetia said with a mysterious smile. "Or I might have another trick up my sleeve."

"That one will do very well," he said, entirely failing to appreciate the hint she was giving him.

She started to speak, then checked herself and fell silent, with a little smile on her face.

At last it was time to depart. The band, which had

followed them to the station, now played the National Anthem again as the train pulled out.

Then it was time for lunch in the luxuriously appointed saloon car, with waiters hovering, anxious to know if the food and wines were to their liking.

It crossed Venetia's mind that, at this moment, she might have been sitting alone in her house in England, wondering what was to become of her.

Instead she was in India, on the most exciting journey of her life, in the company of the most wickedly attractive man she had ever known. She was heading for a thrilling future, all the more thrilling for being completely unknown.

When it grew late, she bade the men goodnight and walked ahead to the room she would share with her husband.

Except that he was not yet really her husband. After the first night, when he had seemed ready to assert his rights by force, he had treated her with the utmost respect. At first she had been glad of that, but increasingly the thought was slipping into her head that perhaps he was being too respectful.

It was almost as though he did not want her after all.

Perhaps he was seriously considering a parting when this trip was over?

At that thought her heart gave a sudden lurch and she was aware of a feeling of anguish, as though parting from him would be the most painful thing that could ever happen to her.

Was it possible that she was in love with him?

She tried to tell herself that this was impossible.

Who could love such an awkward, arrogant man, so sharp-tongued and unreasonable, so dictatorial?

But then her sense of fairness intervened. He had been like that at first, but now his manner to her had grown gentler, even a little humorous. This was fertile soil in which love could flourish.

But after the first night he had made no further move to become her lover. He helped her dress and undress with hands as impersonal as a maid's. At night he kissed her cheek and retired without so much as a backward look.

Respect?

Or indifference?

What would he do tonight?

A soft knock on the door told her that he had arrived. He entered the bedroom, arrayed in a crimson velvet dressing gown, having changed in his valet's room.

"I thought you might need my aid to remove your dress," he said.

"Thank you," she said, trying to sound normal, although her heart had started to thump.

She felt his fingers unlacing her at the back and tensed herself with anticipation. But there was only the rush of air on her skin as the dress loosened. Then his voice came from the door.

"I'll leave you now and return when you are in bed."

When he had departed she pulled off the rest of her clothes. For some reason she was perilously close to being in a really impressive temper.

She lay in bed, her face turned to the wall, refusing to let him think she minded, or even noticed, whether or not he had returned.

At last she heard the sound of the door quietly opening and closing. There was a slight creak as he got into his bed and then the light went out.

Venetia lay in the darkness, listening to the sound of his slow even breathing, until at last she realised that he had fallen asleep.

She sat up in bed and looked over at him. In the darkness she could just make out that he was lying with his back to her, not moving.

There was nothing for her to do but lie down again and try, grumpily, to go to sleep. Which she did.

When she awoke she could see some light coming in through the gaps in the curtains over the windows. Gently she pulled aside the curtain to look outside. What she saw made her sit up sharply and stare out of the window.

Never in her life had she seen such magnificence. Mountains reared up before her and even in the grey dawn light she could see that they were dramatic and strongly coloured. The pallid light of England had never shown her anything like this.

She watched as trees, shrubs and flowers swept past her in brilliant glory. Had there ever been a country like this, she wondered? Intense. Glorious.

She was so entranced that she became oblivious to anything else, barely hearing the movements behind her. Only when the Earl's hands descended lightly on her shoulders did she realise that he had left his bed and come to join her.

"It's magnificent, isn't it?" he asked.

"I had no idea," she murmured. "It's even more glorious than I dreamed."

"Yes it is," he replied softly.

He was sitting on the bed just behind her. His body barely touched hers, but it was enough to make her intensely aware that she was wearing only a thin nightdress. She wondered if he too was thinking of the fact that she had nothing on beneath it. And if so, did that thought tempt him? Did she sense a faint tremor go through his body? Could he sense the tremor in hers?

Perhaps he did, because he turned her gently so that

she lay in his arms, her loosened hair flowing over her shoulders. He stroked it with light fingers before lowering his head so that his lips just touched hers.

She felt herself soften and grow warm under that kiss. It was gentle, tender, waiting for her response and suddenly she felt safe. Her hands seemed to find their own way, touching his face, his hair.

He drew back a moment to look down into her eyes, silently asking her a question. She gave him her answer with a smile.

"My wife," he whispered.

"Yes."

And after that there were no more words, only the strength of his embrace, and the fierce beauty of becoming truly his wife at last.

When they awoke again several hours had passed. Venetia found herself still lying in his arms in the narrow bed.

As before he was smiling at her, but this was a different smile. Last night they had found each other. Now they shared something that she dared to call love.

He had not said that he loved her, but she was content to wait for that. She had seen the look in his eyes, the tenderness in his embrace and for now that was enough.

He drew her out of the bed and held her close for a moment before saying,

"There's something I want you to have."

He reached into a leather bag on the floor, and drew out the engagement ring that she had returned to him so defiantly on the first day of their marriage.

"Now it is right that you should wear my mother's ring," he said. "I hope you will accept it."

"I would love to wear it," she said, and he slipped it

onto her finger.

She felt as though they had reached their true beginning.

But who knew what the end would be?

At last they reached Calcutta and the train drew slowly into the station. Again there was a band playing, and when Venetia looked out of the window she saw flags flying.

It suddenly became very real to her. They were here as the honoured guests of the Viceroy, the Queen's representative. And for a while they too were to be treated like Royalty.

"My Lord," she said suddenly.

He took her hand.

"Don't you think, after last night, you could call me Ivan?"

"Of course," she said, blushing slightly as the memory came back to her.

"Let me hear you say my name."

"Ivan," she whispered.

"What did you want to say to me?"

If he had been hoping for some expression of romantic devotion, he was to be disappointed. Venetia said calmly,

"I wanted to ask if you'd ever been to Kedleston Hall?"

"I beg your pardon?" he said blankly. "Did I hear you properly?"

"Yes, I asked if you'd ever been to Kedleston Hall in England. It's the home of the Curzon family."

"Yes. I had dinner there once. But what of it. My dear Venetia, have you been affected by the sun?"

She laughed.

"No, I promise you. It's just that when we reach Raj Bhavan, the Viceroy's residence, you may find it familiar. I read somewhere that when it was built, sixty years ago, the architect imitated Kedleston Hall."

She saw him looking sceptical and laughed again.

"All right, don't believe me. Just wait until you see."

Someone knocked on their door. It was time for them to leave the train. As she collected her bag Venetia whispered,

"The architect was Captain Charles Wyatt, a Bengal engineer."

Her husband gave her a sideways look. Then the door was pulled open, and there was no chance for further conversation. From now on they were 'on duty'.

CHAPTER EIGHT

They stepped down from the train onto a red carpet, where a man wearing a coat covered in gilt braid was waiting for them. He introduced himself as the Honourable Charles Edmonds and in a loud voice, welcomed them on behalf of the Viceroy.

The Earl made the necessary responses, after which the young man led them to the carriage that was waiting to take them to Raj Bhavan, the Viceregal mansion.

It was not a long journey. They travelled through streets lined with people who cheered and waved when they saw the Royal crest on the sides of the carriages.

The Earl acknowledged the cheers and suggested that Venetia did the same. She waved and smiled, feeling very strange. Inside herself she was still ordinary Venetia Baydon, living in a backwater, known to nobody.

But in fact she was the Countess of Mountwood, the guest of the Queen's representative. And she must play her part. So she too smiled and waved.

"I will look forward to telling Her Majesty what a warm welcome we received on her behalf," the Earl told the Honourable Charles.

"Queen Victoria is very popular in India," he replied. "When the Viceroy entertains guests from England, the whole town seems to go mad."

At last they approached a pair of high wrought iron gates that immediately swung open to admit the stream of carriages. In another few moments they were at the start of the long drive, their view filled by the great white palatial house, the front dominated by tall slender pillars.

As the carriage drew up, the Viceroy and Vicereine emerged from the house and descended the stairs.

Lord Lytton was a tall, elegant man in his late forties, with fine features, dark hair and a long dark curly beard. His wife, about ten years his junior, was equally elegant with a slightly haughty air, but a lovely smile.

"Mountwood," the Viceroy said, seizing his guest's hand. "So glad to meet you at last. Her Majesty has written a great deal to me about you. She praises you to the skies."

When he greeted Venetia, he gave her a shrewd look that made her wonder exactly what he had heard. It occurred to her that he might have been given Mary's name. She caught the Earl's eye and knew that he was thinking the same thing. Fortunately neither the Viceroy nor his wife made any awkward comments.

From the moment of their arrival they were enveloped in luxury. Since Venetia had no maid with her, Lady Lytton offered the use of her own. Now she could bask in the pleasure of being really well looked after.

Having shown her personally to her suite, the Vicereine then took her on a tour of that part of the palace that was used as a residence, the rest being given over to the Royal Court.

She was in her thirties with a face that was still pretty, although the birth of seven children in fourteen years, with two sons dead in infancy, had left her a little worn.

But just now her mood was cheerful. She had borne another son earlier that year, and she glowed with happiness as she showed Venetia the nursery.

'Will this happen to me?' Venetia thought. 'To bear children to your husband, then see them die and go on to have more. Only the greatest love could make it endurable.'

Lady Lytton noticed her pensive mood and put it down to the strain of the journey.

"You are tired," she said. "Let us return to your apartment, and you must take all the time you need to prepare for tonight."

While Clarice, the maid, unpacked and hung up her clothes, Venetia was free to lie back in a bath, feeling the heat and strain of the journey float away from her.

Now she felt well, relaxed and ready to play her part in this glittering scene.

It was time to dress for dinner. She chose one of her new gowns from Gibraltar, a wonderful creation of rose silk and gauze, decorated with tiny velvet rosebuds and dainty satin ribbons.

There was a knock on her door. The maid admitted the Earl, curtsied and departed.

"You look beautiful," he told Venetia, his eyes warm and appreciative. "But when we return home it will be my pleasure to take you to Paris, and have the couturiers dress you as your beauty deserves to be dressed."

"You don't think I do you credit now?" she asked demurely.

"I have already told you that you look beautiful," he said, smiling.

"Ah, I see!"

"What do you see, madam? I mistrust that ironic tone of yours. It means you're going to say something disconcerting."

"I was only thinking that you're going to be the kind of husband who rations his compliments. Perhaps you think I may become vain?"

The Earl's answer to this was to seize her in his arms and cover her mouth in a fierce crushing kiss. For a long moment the world spun giddily while his lips moved over hers, teasing and coaxing.

"That is what I think of you," he said at last, gasping slightly. "And let that be a lesson to you not to ask foolish questions."

Venetia's eyes gleamed with amusement – and something else.

"I don't think any further questions will be necessary, my Lord." she observed. She too was gasping a little.

His eyes gleamed in return, understanding her message perfectly.

"Little witch," he said amiably. "Now stop tempting me and attend to serious business."

He picked up a box which he had brought into the room and had then set down hurriedly while he kissed her.

"I brought some of my mother's jewels with me," he said. "Tonight I should like you to wear her pearls."

He draped a triple string about her neck and placed a pearl tiara on her head. Every pearl was perfect and she knew the worth of them all must be fabulous.

"I'm nervous," she said suddenly. "I know nothing about this kind of life. Suppose I let you down."

"You won't let me down," he said gently. "Just be your normal beautiful clever self, and everyone will admire you as I do."

Admire, she noticed. Not love.

Together they descended the huge staircase to be greeted by their hosts, who explained that they would dine privately tonight, because nobody had known exactly when they would arrive.

But now messages had been sent out and tomorrow

night there would be a formidable array of guests to greet them.

The 'private' dining room turned out to be a vast room with walls lined with tables groaning with side dishes. In the centre a table was laid for five, Lord and Lady Lytton, Lord and Lady Mountwood, and Lord Anthony.

The meal was splendid beyond anything Venetia had imagined. The gleaming white china bore the Royal crest, which was also on the heavy crystal glasses and every piece of the gold cutlery.

Servants glided silently back and forth offering food and the very best wines.

It was delightful to be treated like this, but Venetia was conscious of being under scrutiny by people who wanted to know if she could live up to her position.

Then she realised that the Earl was also under scrutiny. Lord Lytton was engaging him in deep conversation about the situation on the North-West frontier and, in particular, about the Treaty of Gandamark, which the Viceroy had concluded earlier that year with the Emir of Afghanistan.

Listening closely, Venetia discovered that, in return for an annual payment of six hundred thousand rupees, the Emir guaranteed the safety of British subjects going about their lawful business, especially trade.

"Will the Emir keep his side of the Treaty?" the Earl wanted to know.

"Oh, he's a good fellow, he will do his best," the Viceroy replied. "But that doesn't mean the Russians on his frontier will give him any peace. They'll try to force him to break the treaty or make it look as if he's broken it, and try to provoke us into reaction."

"In that case," said the Earl, "it seems to me that what we must do – "

The conversation became military and detailed. To

Venetia's great pleasure her husband showed himself knowledgeable. He seemed to have the whole area fixed in his brain, plus which troops were stationed where, and what they were doing.

She had thought that Lord Anthony, exquisite in full evening dress, would be out of his depth in this discussion. But he surprised her by being knowledgable, particularly on the subject of the tribesmen who regularly crossed the India-Afghan border, and who often turned out to be British soldiers in disguise.

"Dashed exciting thing to do," he said. "Always thought I'd like to try it myself."

There was a stunned silence during which the others tried to imagine this willowy, delicate young man in tribesman's clothes. And failed.

"Just a thought," he said defensively, as they all burst into laughter.

"Keep it as a thought, old fellow," the Earl advised him in an unsteady voice. "Never try to spoil the fantasy with reality."

"Oh, I say!" said Anthony, his feelings hurt.

The talk passed onto other matters, nearer home.

"I wonder if you've had time to form an opinion of Raj Bhavan," Lady Lytton said to the Earl.

"Magnificent," he replied at once. "In fact it's as splendid as I would expect in a Royal residence."

There was a slight pause in which Venetia could sense him trying to make up his mind. She saw his tension and then he relaxed as he decided to take a risk.

"At the same time," he said, "it has an air of comfort that reminds me of the best sort of English country house."

"I wonder why you should say that," Lady Lytton teased.

"I understand, ma'am, that it was modelled after Kedleston Hall, home of the Curzon family, and where I have had the pleasure of dining."

"I'm glad to find you so well informed," Lord Lytton said, sounding pleased. "Does your knowledge extend to the name of the architect?"

The Earl took a deep breath, like a man about to dive off a high ledge into a deep ocean.

"I believe it was Captain Charles Wyatt, a Bengal engineer," he said.

There was a murmur of approval from the Viceroy and his lady.

"It isn't often that our visitors are so well rounded in their knowledge of India," Lord Lytton said. "I had expected you to know about the frontier, but for you to know the history of this building as well is a bonus. I congratulate you."

Across the table the Earl's eyes briefly met Venetia's and he raised his glass to her in a gesture of salute.

But she had yet another surprise for him, as he was about to discover.

"And you ma'am," the Viceroy said, turning to her. "Are you as well versed in this country as Lord Mountwood."

"I am afraid not," she said meekly. "I do not aspire to my husband's level of learning."

The Earl had the grace to blush.

"I spend much of my time reading poetry," Venetia continued. "I am particularly fond of the works of Owen Meredith. In fact, *Lucile* has long been my favourite poem."

There was a sudden silence. Venetia's eyes met Lord Lytton's and found a question in them. She answered it by quoting the first few lines of the long, narrative poem that had taken the literary world by storm a few years earlier.

"You *knew!*" the Viceroy said.

"I must admit that I did know," she confessed. "But truly, I have always been an admirer of Mr. Meredith."

The Viceroy gave a sudden roar of laughter.

"Well done, ma'am!" he said. "You have taken me completely by surprise."

The Earl was looking from one to the other as the truth dawned on him.

"My Lord," Venetia said to him, "allow me to introduce Mr. Owen Meredith."

The Viceroy gave an ironic bow. Lady Lytton was laughing with delight.

"Now you have really pleased him," she confided to Venetia. "There's nothing Edward likes more than to be admired for his poetry."

"Mountwood, I congratulate you," the Viceroy said. "Your wife belongs in the diplomatic corps. You have made an excellent choice."

"I agree," the Earl said, his smiling eyes on Venetia.

By common consent they all retired early, to be prepared for the long day ahead.

When the maid had departed Venetia lay in the darkness, waiting for the sound she longed to hear, the click of the door latch. At last it came. She felt Ivan slip into the bed beside her and the next moment she was enfolded in his arms.

Later, as they lay contentedly together he said, in an amused voice,

"If you wanted to take me by surprise tonight, you succeeded. Who would have dreamed he was a poet?"

"Yes, he doesn't look like one with that beard, does he?" she said.

"How lucky that you should have admired his work so much."

"Well – " she said cautiously.

"What does that mean? You said *Lucile* was your favourite poem."

"It was, when I first read it. But I was only sixteen. It's all about a pair of lovers who are separated in youth and meet up again when they're old, and she's become a nun."

She lowered her voice to a whisper and said in his ear,

"You never read such sentimental nonsense in your life. But naturally I couldn't say that to him."

There was a stunned silence. Then he roared with laughter. When he was calm again, he took her hand and laid it against his lips, saying

"He said you belonged in the diplomatic corps and he didn't know how right he was."

Then he was drawing her close again, murmuring,

"My love – my love – "

And they forgot all about the Viceroy and his poetry. They forgot about everything in the world but each other.

*

For Venetia the following day was taken up with visits to a hospital and a school in the company of Lady Lytton. Then it was time to return to Raj Bhavan to prepare for the great banquet that was to be given in their honour that evening.

If she had dressed with care the night before, Venetia knew that she must be a thousand times more careful now. Tonight they would be 'on display'.

She wore a white satin brocade gown swept back into an elaborate bustle. She had half planned to wear the pearls again, but the Earl insisted that this time it must be diamonds.

"Ready?" he asked her.

She took a deep breath.

"I'm ready for anything."

He offered her his arm and they walked out together. A Major Domo was waiting for them, to escort them to their seats as the guests of honour.

Venetia nearly gasped aloud at the sight of the company. There must have been at least five hundred guests, all summoned at a day's notice.

But of course, she realised, this was a 'Royal' household and everyone would be flattered to be invited, even at the last minute.

At last the trumpets blared and the Viceroy and Vicereine made their entrance, to the sound of the National Anthem. They took their places in the centre of the top table and the banquet began.

Venetia found that there was too much space between her and the person sitting next to her to allow of much conversation. But she soon realised that the real point of being here was to allow herself to be studied.

After a while she managed to relax, and enjoyed studying the others. As the top table was on a raised dais, she had a good view of all the other guests.

There were many army officers, splendid in dress uniform. The top level of court officials was also well represented.

There were also many guests who were obviously members of India's aristocracy. The women were beautiful, adorned with rubies and emeralds that glowed against their brilliantly coloured clothes. The men were magnificent and also adorned with jewels.

After a very long banquet, of many courses, and a confusing multitude of different wines, it was time for the speeches.

The Viceroy welcomed his honoured guests who had come all the way from England as a sign of Her Majesty's affection. Then the Earl made a speech in which he praised the Queen and the Viceroy as Her Majesty's representative in India.

It seemed to Venetia that the speeches went on forever. This was certainly not the kind of adventurous life that she had anticipated. She was relieved when it was time to dance.

Even then there was a formality about matters that oppressed her. First she danced with the Viceroy, followed by his deputy and then with all the most important guests.

Finally she was free to pick her own partners and she found a crowd of good-looking young officers begging to dance with her.

"I say, what fun it will be having you here with us," one of them said as they waltzed.

"But I don't know how long I'm going to be here."

"Well, at least until Lord Mountwood gets back from the frontier. We're all longing to show you around."

"Hmm!" she murmured thoughtfully.

In the same moment she saw her husband dancing by. He was looking at her and scowling. Then she realised that the young officer was holding her improperly close and looking down at her with an infatuated expression.

The evening was finally over. The guests dispersed and she was free to go to bed, enjoyably weary and full of thought.

There was a great deal to ponder, plans to make.

When her husband entered he found her sitting before her mirror attired in a floaty gauze creation that suited her so admirably that for a moment he was struck silent.

His next action was to lean down and kiss the back of her neck.

Only then did he recall that he had come to reprove her.

"I thought it was quite unnecessary for you to give that young man so much encouragement," he ventured.

"What you mean?" she asked in genuine confusion. There had been so many dancing partners that they had all blended into one.

"You know very well which one I mean. He was leaning over you and yearning in the most theatrical way."

"Well, I could hardly push him off in the middle of a ballroom, could I? Besides, our soldiers are the backbone of the Empire. They should be encouraged, not repulsed."

"When an upstart young fellow starts making eyes at my wife, I expect her to repulse him. Let that be clear to you madam."

"He wasn't making eyes at me. Well, maybe just a little bit, but in a very gentlemanly fashion."

"He was holding you improperly close."

"Only to make sure that I could hear him properly above the music. He was telling me about your plan to go North."

"Of course. You always knew I was going to the frontier."

"Without me?"

"It will be a long, tiring and dangerous journey. No place for a woman. You'll be much better off here."

"I most certainly will not. I'm not spending all my time making official visits and sitting through interminable speeches while you have all the fun."

"Fun? First we have a long train journey to Lahore. Then we go by horseback through the Khyber Pass, between some of the most bare and inhospitable mountains in the world. You call that fun?"

"It sounds more fun than staying here being bored," she said defiantly. "I'm coming with you."

"You are not."

"I am."

"You will stay here in safety."

"That won't suit me at all."

"You are my wife and you will obey me."

For a moment the air soured, as they squared up to each other. Then, abruptly, Venetia's hostility faded and she smiled sweetly at him.

"Of course I will. What was I thinking of? I will obey you in everything."

"You will?" he asked, regarding her with well-founded suspicion.

"Of course I will. I'm sure I'll find plenty of things to do here. After all, Captain Fitzhoon said they were all looking forward to showing me around."

"Captain who?"

"Captain Fitzhoon, the young man you saw me dancing with. I've just remembered his name. Or was he the other one? That's right. It was Major Langley I was dancing with and Captain Fitzhoon who's going to take me on a picnic. I get confused because they're all so fine and handsome, but I'll learn their names soon – riding with them and dancing with them and – "

"You will do no such thing," her husband said through gritted teeth. "You are coming to the frontier with me."

"Yes, dear," she said meekly.

"And take that gleam out of your eye."

"Yes, dear."

"And come to bed."

"Yes, dear."

They set off next day in the Royal train, travelling from Calcutta to Jhelum in the north.

"What exactly does the Queen want you to do?" Venetia asked.

"Study the military situation, and see if we have enough troops in the area for both official and unofficial duties."

"Unofficial? You mean pretending to be tribesmen?" she asked eagerly.

"I say, yes!" Anthony said at once.

"Will the two of you please stop that? We're embarked on the serious business of assessing the Russian threat."

"Of course we are," Venetia said gravely.

"Although frankly" the Earl replied, "I think as soon as the Russians hear that you've arrived they'll withdraw back to Moscow. At least, they will if they have any sense."

Venetia chuckled.

They spent the next two days travelling through the most savagely beautiful scenery she had ever seen. Mountains, greenery and flowers lined their way, all in the most brilliant colours.

At last they pulled into Jhelum, which was as far as the train went. After that they would go on horseback to Peshawar for the entrance to the Khyber Pass.

A contingent of soldiers was waiting to greet them. They looked surprised at the sight of Venetia, but surprise changed to delight when they saw how pretty she was.

"Don't worry ma'am, we'll protect you," one of them said.

"Are we likely to encounter trouble?" the Earl asked.

"One never knows what those devils are up to, my Lord," came the reply. "The other night, when I went out to get a breath of fresh air, I found there were quite a number of hostile creatures trying to set fire to the fort. We are quite certain it was a band of Russians, who had suggested they should burn us to death as they were unable to shoot us."

"I say!" Anthony murmured.

The Earl turned abruptly to Venetia.

"I think – "

"It's too late to send me back now," she told him. "Come on. The sooner we start the better."

The soldiers cheered her, and it was a merry party that went on its way.

All except for the Earl. When he considered the danger into which he might be leading Venetia, he remembered the glow in the eyes of the young officers and he was not sure which worried him more.

CHAPTER NINE

At last they reached the fort at Peshawar and beyond lay the Khyber Pass.

Here the land was very bleak and lonely. Even the fort seemed forbidding, a large grey building that loomed up ahead, seeming to offer more of a threat than a welcome.

Scanning the walls Venetia saw gaps in the bricks, through which huge guns could be glimpsed.

"We keep the cannon ready to repel attack at all times," said the young officer riding beside her. "There are three facing the Pass and one on each of the other sides."

"They look so grim," she murmured.

"They do, but they keep us safe. The Russians know they're there and it makes them cautious, ma'am. In fact, you could almost say that life gets dull sometimes. It's a great treat when visitors arrive."

She soon discovered how true that was, as they reached the fort and received an excited and enthusiastic welcome.

They were greeted by eight officers who took them immediately into the fort itself, where food and drink were waiting for them.

The Commanding Officer introduced himself as Colonel Arkwright.

"You are very brave to come here," he told Venetia.

"It's not often that ladies are sufficiently intrepid to struggle over these rough roads."

"I think you are wonderful to hold back the enemy so effectively," Venetia said.

The Colonel smiled at her.

"Well, we are always kept on our toes, so to speak, but some of the stories which go south are exaggerated and it's not as bad as they pretend."

"You should be very proud to have kept the fort in our hands," the Earl said. "I want to explain to Her Majesty how brave you are being and how successfully you have kept the Russians at bay. Although I expect they will go on trying."

The Colonel laughed.

"They never give in," he replied. "We have to be alert night and day. At the same time they don't attack us as frequently as they did when I first came here."

The Earl inspected all the soldiers on duty, not only in the fort itself, but in tents in a compound outside the walls.

"You have more men than I expected," he commented when they returned to the fort.

"I insist on having enough troops," Colonel Arkwright told him. "Although it's a rough and hard life, those down in the south all seem to wish to join us sooner or later."

"Yes, I remember my own army days," the Earl mused. "Especially the excitement of action."

As he said this he looked up to see Venetia coming towards him and grinned at her. But she did not smile back. There had been something in his voice that told her he wanted to be in the thick of it.

And he must not do that, she thought wildly. He must not risk his life just when she was discovering how much he meant to her. She could not endure it.

She wondered how the other women managed. There

were several ladies at the fort, as the higher ranking officers were allowed to have their wives with them. They seemed to live serenely, dividing their time between domestic affairs and helping out in the fort hospital.

The Colonel's lady took Venetia under her wing. She was kind and pleasant, but Venetia would rather have been listening to the men.

That evening the officers entertained them to a feast. She found herself sitting far apart from the Earl and there was no chance to talk to him.

Later he suggested that she must be weary after the long journey and everyone would understand if she retired. This she understood to mean that he wanted her to leave, so that he could talk freely with the men.

There was nothing for it but to do as he wished. She said goodnight graciously to conceal the fact that she was seething inside and departed.

It was another three hours before the Earl joined her.

"I'm sorry if I disturbed you," he said.

"I wasn't asleep," she said truthfully. She had been lying awake, worrying.

She heard him undress and get into bed beside her.

"Are you tired?" he asked in the tender voice that always made her heart beat faster.

But she refused to yield to it.

"I'd like to talk," she said firmly.

In the darkness she sensed his surprise.

"Very well. What would you like to talk about?"

"About tomorrow, and what we're going to do."

"You might like to visit the fort hospital. I'm sure those poor wounded fellows would appreciate it."

"And what will you be doing?" she asked.

"Exploring the area. I want to take a look at the Khyber Pass."

"Because that's where the Russians come from?"

"It's virtually the only way into India from Afghanistan. We have to keep our eyes on it constantly. But my dear, there is nothing for you to worry about."

"I worry about you. You wish you were back in the army, don't you?"

He gave a grin that was almost sheepish.

"Well, perhaps I do – just a little."

"But you are not in the army," she said fiercely. "Fighting the Russians is their business, not yours. Remember you have to return to England and report to the Queen. You mustn't risk your life. It belongs to *her.*"

"Are you sure you don't mean that it belongs to you?" he asked.

She tensed, hearing in his tone an accusation of possessiveness.

"Certainly not," she said quickly. "I would never burden you with claims for myself."

In the dim light she could not see the look that passed across his face. It might have been one of disappointment. `

"Let us go to sleep," he said. "Tomorrow will be a busy day."

"Yes," she replied in a colourless voice. "Goodnight."

She lay listening to the sound of his breathing, until at last she could tell that he was asleep. Slowly she sat up and looked down at his face, which she could just discern.

In sleep he looked completely relaxed and untroubled, and she realised that whatever went on in his head was hidden from her.

In one sense they had grown close, but at this moment she discovered the limits of that closeness. He could still shut her out, leaving her with no clue as to what he was thinking.

And she wanted everything. Passion was not enough. She wanted to be the companion of his mind as well as his heart, and she was a long way from that.

It was as though she had been travelling down a long road, confident that she had almost reached her destination, only to discover that the gate she had thought led to home, merely opened onto a distant and far more complicated journey.

On this thought she fell asleep.

She awoke to find herself alone. Through the cracks in the curtains she could see that the sun was brilliant.

The door opened quietly, and Mrs. Arkwright, the Colonel's wife, looked in, smiling and coming into the room when she saw that Venetia was awake.

"Your husband said you were not to be disturbed," she said. "So we let you sleep off the rigours of your travels."

"Oh – thank you. Is it very late?"

"Nearly ten o'clock."

"Goodness, I must get up. Ivan will think I'm going to sleep forever."

"Don't worry. He isn't here. My husband is showing him the Khyber Pass."

"But isn't that very dangerous?"

"They have a troop of soldiers with them. Lord Anthony went too. They'll probably be back tomorrow."

"Probably? Tomorrow?" Venetia echoed, aghast.

"They'll stay away overnight, I dare say. Don't worry. I have lots of things to keep you amused."

She seemed to think that this solved every problem, but Venetia knew a sudden, devastating sense of betrayal.

Ivan had crept away while she slept, and she knew why. It was so that she would not 'make a fuss'. She was only a woman and women did not understand military matters. It was better to keep the little dears in the dark until the men had escaped.

He had even taken Anthony, a charming creature but as useless a specimen of manhood as it was possible to imagine.

Venetia wanted to throw something.

Somehow she got through the day that followed. When evening came there was no sign of the men returning. She joined the other women for dinner, and although they expressed conventional concern it was clear that they saw nothing unusual in the matter.

"My husband is sometimes away for weeks at a time," Mrs. Arkwright said. "But he always returns."

"And you're not frightened?" Venetia asked.

"Of course, but you soon grow used to it."

Venetia did not think she would ever grow used to it. She would happily have braved any danger at her husband's side, but to know that he was out there in the darkness was terrible to her.

She lay awake all that night, veering between fear for her husband and anger against him for slipping away without telling her.

In the morning there was still no sign of him. It was late afternoon before the party returned and when she saw him again she had a shock.

Before her stood a man in scruffy old rags, a turban around his head and a dirty scarf covering the lower part of his face. Only his eyes were unmistakeably the Earl's.

"Hello," he said, pulling the scarf away and grinning at her.

"You!" she said explosively.

Beside him another tribesman, equally shabby, shouted with laughter.

"I say," he said.

"Anthony? You too?"

"It's been a great day," Anthony said cheerfully. "Well, except for poor Devenish. He had a bad fall."

Their injured comrade was being hurriedly taken into the hospital.

Venetia seized her husband's hand.

"Come with me," she said.

"I have to report to the Colonel first – "

"Come with me."

He gave up protesting and allowed her to drag him inside and up to their room.

"It was terrible of me to go off like that, wasn't it?" he said, but although his words were contrite his eyes were gleaming with fun.

"It was monstrous," she said, in a fury now that she knew he was safe. "It was wicked, it was unspeakable."

That was all she was able to say. The Earl's arms closed around her with crushing force.

Her first instinct was to be angry. How dare he think he could simply overwhelm her like this when she was rightly angry with him.

With all her mind she tried to resist the effect he had on her, but the feel of his lips moving over hers drove all other thoughts from her head. Now there was nothing in her but feeling.

The sensations, both physical and emotional, that he knew so well how to induce in her, were rising, engulfing her, until she had no will but his.

"Do you know how much I've missed you?" he whispered.

She could only shake her head dumbly, while her pulses raced.

"Then let me show you," he said, lifting her and carrying her towards the bed.

*

Lieutenant Devenish had a broken leg. He would recover, but he would be out of action for some time.

"And that is awkward," the Colonel confided over supper that evening, "because he speaks fluent Russian. We have nobody else with such a skill."

"And I believe he was on the verge of a great discovery," the Earl said. "There's a small Russian camp about fifteen miles along the Pass. We managed to get close enough to overhear them talking and Devenish was getting excited."

"Didn't he tell you what they were saying?" the Colonel asked anxiously.

"He had no chance. There was a commotion from inside the tent – some kind of a quarrel I think – and they started to get close to us. We beat a hasty retreat, but the ground was rough and Devenish's horse stumbled and threw him.

"We managed to remount him and get away, but the poor fellow was in agony, half fainting most of the way."

"And he's in a high fever now," Mrs. Arkwright added. "We won't get any sense out of him for a while, poor fellow."

"And that's serious," said the Colonel, "because whatever he heard was obviously important. We shall just have to pray that he recovers consciousness quickly."

He turned to Anthony.

"What sort of a time did you have, sir? A bit rough, was it?"

"Never had a better time in my life," Anthony said

unexpectedly.

"What, dressed in those terrible clothes?" Venetia asked.

"All part of the fun," he said at once.

"He really did enjoy himself," the Earl said. "I was astonished.

"And we'll have to go back," Anthony said at once. "If Devenish doesn't come round and tell us what he learned, we can't leave it there."

"No," the Colonel said strongly. "But let's hope he improves."

He did not improve, however. By next morning his fever had climbed dangerously, and he could do nothing but toss and turn, raving incoherently.

"Last thing – expect – " he gasped. "Take them by surprise – English devils – *English devils* – "

"I suppose that means us," the Colonel said wryly. "He's repeating something he heard, but heaven knows what it can be. And how can they take us by surprise when we're always on full alert for an attack?"

"Then it's something we haven't thought of," the Earl said heavily. "But in heaven's name, *what?*"

"I can't begin to imagine," replied the Colonel.

Devenish groaned. Venetia seated herself on his bed and gently mopped his brow. He was still talking, but his voice had dropped to a mutter.

"Look, Colonel, we can't wait any longer," the Earl said. "We have to go back to that camp and find what else there is to learn."

"But how?" the Colonel demanded. "I have nobody else here who can speak Russian. That was Devenish's special value to us."

"Nobody else?" the Earl echoed, aghast.

"Some of the lads have picked up a smattering, but we've nobody who speaks it fluently like him. There was one other man but he was killed and I'm still waiting for a replacement. You might tell Her Majesty that, Lord Mountwood."

"I will, but it doesn't help us much now," he replied heavily.

Suddenly Devenish sat up in bed, screaming the same three words over and over again. Then abruptly he stopped and fell back on the bed, his chest heaving, his eyes staring wildly.

"That sounded like Russian," the Colonel said. "But what the devil was he saying?"

"He was saying, 'Kill them all, kill them all,'" Venetia said quietly.

In the stunned silence that followed, they turned to look at her.

"You understood that?" the Colonel asked.

"Oh yes. I speak Russian. I had a governess whose mother was Russian. She taught it to me. She said I ought to know a better language than insipid English. I've always loved it."

She rose and stood between the Earl and the Colonel, looking from one to the other.

"It's going to have to be me."

"You can forget that," the Earl rapped out. "There is simply no way that I'll allow you to go through the Pass to find the Russian camp."

"But why not?" she asked with an air of honest surprise.

"Why not? Isn't it obvious?"

"Not to me. You came here to do a job for your country. Now you find there's only one way of doing it, you can't refuse that one way. It would be to fail in your duty."

He stared at her.

"Ivan, listen," she said urgently. "The Russians have a secret that can destroy this place and everyone in it. If they succeed it could put the whole North-West frontier at risk.

"It doesn't matter that I am a woman. It doesn't matter that I am your wife. What matters is that you've been shown a way to avoid disaster. An instrument has been put into your hand, and you must use that instrument. You have no choice."

In his horrified silence and deadly pallor, she saw that he had understood the truth of this.

"She's right," the Colonel said quietly. "What would the Queen expect of us?"

"She would expect us to take any risk, no matter what the cost," the Earl said in a hollow voice.

"I think we should make a start at once," Venetia said. "Then we can approach them by night."

There was nothing more to say. The Earl knew that she was right. It was their duty to their country to take any risk, at any sacrifice to themselves.

He had always believed that, but never before had the potential sacrifice been so great. He wanted to cry out that his Venetia must not be subject to danger because he could not live without her.

Instead, he said bleakly,

"You are right, my love. Let us be gone as soon as possible."

"You'll take a contingent with you," the Colonel said. "They'll make sure you come back safely."

"Thank you," Venetia said quietly.

But they all knew that she was on a mission that only she could accomplish, that there would come a moment when she must face danger alone, when, perhaps, nobody could guarantee her safety.

As they walked back to their room, the Earl went through the things he would like to say to her, but he found he could say none of them.

He no longer recognised her. He had not known that she spoke Russian, but then, he wondered, how well had he ever known her?

The cheerful, sharp-witted girl who had snared his interest and then his heart had vanished, replaced by this steely young woman who had made her decision without asking his opinion.

"It doesn't matter that I am your wife."

She had said that. Did she mean it?

Almost as soon as they reached their room, there was a knock on the door and it was Mrs. Arkwright, bearing a set of tribesmen's clothes.

"Luckily you're fairly tall," she said. "So I think you'll find them a good fit. They're really quite clean, considering."

"Shall I help you put them on?" the Earl asked, when they were alone again.

"Yes, please."

He played 'lady's maid' for her, as he had done many times before, but this time it was different. This time one or both of them might not come back alive.

He removed her dress, helped her on with the ragged trousers and long tunic and then wrapped the turban around her head.

He dressed himself in his own rags and rubbed some brown boot polish into his face.

"Now it's your turn," he said. "Anyone who lives here soon gets a deep tan, so we must hide our light skins or they would soon realise we are strangers. Mind you, I hope we may manage to pass unseen."

She stood still while he darkened her face, looking up at him with a faint smile on her face.

"I won't let anything happen to you," he said fervently.

"Nothing can happen to me if I'm with you," Venetia replied simply.

He put his arms around her, drawing her close and holding her in a fierce hug. She held him in return, each of them wondering if they would ever share a moment like this again.

This was not the right time for a declaration of love and there was no need for words. Each felt the strength of the emotional bond that held them fast.

There was a knock on the door.

"We're gathering downstairs," came the Colonel's voice.

"We're coming," Venetia called.

They left the room hand in hand, heading down to the courtyard where a group of soldiers, all dressed as tribesmen, stood by their horses. When they saw Venetia, they sent up a spontaneous cheer and burst into applause.

The Earl joined in the applause, regarding his wife with pride. Anthony too was applauding, and the two of them stood, one each side of her, while the cheers rose.

Then it was time to leave. The sun was setting fast, dropping down behind the mountains, as they rode out of the great gates of the fort, heading for the Khyber Pass.

The Pass was a very rough road of about thirty miles, starting in the North-West of India and wending its way through the mountains and across the India-Afghan border. On each side rose bleak mountains that were almost impossible to climb, except in a very few places.

As the sun finally disappeared behind the mountains they were plunged into almost total darkness. The little troop moved carefully so as not to make too much noise. Venetia was constantly alert, straining to see any sign of lights that would suggest a camp.

After what seemed like an age they halted. The Major leading the expedition came and spoke quietly.

"We've reached the place where we found the camp last time, and I think we'll see their lights around the next bend. We should dismount here and go softly the rest of the way."

Two soldiers stayed behind with the horses while the rest made their way quietly round the curve in the road, and there in a hollow at the foot of the mountain were the lights of a camp.

Keeping close to the shelter of the mountain, they crept up close to the camp, until they had gone as far as was wise.

"Where was Lieutenant Devenish when he heard something he thought was valuable?" Venetia asked.

The Earl indicated the largest tent. It was well lit and they could discern shadows moving back and forth inside.

"Whoever is in there must be in charge," the Earl whispered.

"Then he's the one who knows the secret," Venetia said softly. "It's time for me to start work."

She glided away from them into the darkness, heading for the large tent. But the Earl was right behind her, determined not to let her out of his sight. Following up to the rear were Anthony and the Major.

There were large rocks to shelter them as they crept round the perimeter of the camp until they reached the large tent. From inside they could clearly hear the sound of voices raised in revelry.

The four of them dropped to the ground, and lay there, listening to the Russians. To the men the words sounded like confusion, but Venetia, listening intently, said at last,

"They're celebrating because they're going to be out of here very soon – they've started packing up already."

"Do they say why they're going?" the Major asked.

She listened for a while, then said,

"They've achieved what they set out to do."

"But don't they say what that was?" the Earl asked urgently.

There was another burst of Russian.

"One of them said, 'we found the right man'," Venetia explained. "And another one keeps saying, 'the die is cast,' and then giving a nasty little giggle."

There was a shout from inside the tent, followed by general laughter.

"Someone said, 'they'll never know what happened'," Venetia told them.

"What do they mean by 'the right man'?" the Major wanted to know. "Have they suddenly found a brilliant new leader."

But Venetia had gone very still.

"No, not that. It's one of our men they're talking about. They've found an English soldier who's helping them."

"A traitor? I don't believe it. You must have misunderstood, ma'am."

"No, I haven't misunderstood. This man is going to sabotage the cannon."

They all exchanged looks of horror.

"Venetia, are you sure?" the Earl asked softly.

"Yes, I'm sure. When the attack comes, the big guns

will be useless, and then they think they can overwhelm us."

"That's what poor Devenish was trying to tell us," Anthony said.

"I refuse to believe it," the Major said stubbornly. "No English soldier would do such a thing."

"Now listen," the Earl told him firmly, "my wife risked her life to get you that information and she's not risking it any further. We're going back to the fort to warn them."

In the face of his fiercely whispered wrath, the Major backed down.

They eased back along the ground until they judged they were far enough away from the tent to risk standing up. Luckily the camp was full of noise and they were able to slip away into the night without being discovered.

On the perimeter they found the soldiers who had accompanied them, and who were becoming anxious.

"To the horses quickly," the Major said. "The sooner we get back to the fort the better."

Once mounted, they moved slowly back down the Pass for the first mile, but then they broke into a gallop. At every moment Venetia expected to hear the sound of Russians pursuing them, but miraculously they made their escape.

As the first dawn light appeared they could make out the huge grey hulk that was the fort. In a few minutes the gates opened to receive them, and they were safely home.

CHAPTER TEN

Colonel Arkwright was relieved and joyful at their safe return, but then appalled when he had heard Venetia's story.

"There's no chance that you could be mistaken?" he asked, more in hope than belief.

"No chance at all," she said. "There's a man in this fort who is working for the Russians, and he's going to disable the cannon so that our strength will be reduced before the attack."

"Thank God you warned us," the Colonel said. "We have time to make sure of the cannon. If anyone tries to get to them, that's our man. And when the attack comes, we'll be ready. You're a true soldier, ma'am. I know no higher praise."

"Thank you," Venetia replied, deeply moved.

But her greatest joy was the glow of pride in her husband's eyes.

"I'll just see my wife to our room," he told the Colonel, "then I'll come back. You'll need every man."

He almost ran with her to their room. There he seized her in his arms and gave her a long, fierce kiss.

"I've never been so frightened in my life," he said. "All the way back I was waiting for an attack, fearful that you would be hurt or killed."

"I was safe while you were with me," she said, thrilled with what she could see in his eyes.

"I shall never let you take such risks again," he said. "From now on – but it's too soon to talk of that yet. First we have to deal with this attack and then we will have time for ourselves."

He kissed her again.

"Go to bed. You've been up all night and you need rest."

She was sure that all the excitement would keep her awake, but when she had taken a bath and slipped between the sheets she found that sleep came easily. The night's exertions had worn her out.

She was awoken by the sound of the door opening and closing as the Earl entered. She could see that the light was fading and she must have slept through most of the day.

"We caught him," he said, sitting on the bed in great excitement. "Colonel Arkwright mounted a treble guard on the cannon, but told them to keep out of sight. They were waiting when the traitor came to disable them."

"But who was it?" she demanded eagerly.

"A man called Kelton. He's a private and, I guess, a thug by nature. He has a grudge because he was constantly passed over for promotion – with good reason, I would imagine. So he sold out to our enemies for gold. He's under arrest now and won't trouble us any further. The guns are safe, and we're ready for the attack."

"And when will it come?"

"Probably tonight. I want you to get dressed and be ready. We should repel them easily, but if not – " he strode over to a cupboard in the corner, unlocked it and took out something which he handled carefully.

"I want you to have this," he said. "Just in case."

Then Venetia saw that he was holding a pistol.

"I'm sure you won't need it," the Earl said reassuringly. "But it will ease my mind in case I can't get here to protect you myself."

They clasped each other tightly, neither able to voice their desperate thoughts. Then he was gone.

Venetia dressed herself hurriedly, trying not to think what might happen.

Looking out of the window, she saw that every man in the fort was on alert for the coming attack. They lined the walls, rifles at the ready.

Suddenly the air was split by the loudest sound she had ever heard. It was the bellow of a cannon and even while she trembled Venetia felt a sense of pride. But for her that cannon might have been silenced.

Then there was more bellowing as the other two cannon facing the front were fired. Distantly she could hear screams as the enemy were mown down, realising that their plan had not succeeded.

Then there was rapid rifle-fire as the soldiers on the walls took up the action.

She wondered where the Earl was, and what he was doing. Had he put himself into the thick of danger?

Desperately she started to pray for him.

The gunfire was getting louder and louder. The roar of the cannon seemed to shake the whole building.

'Let him be safe,' she prayed frantically. 'Please God, save him.'

She said the same words over and over, while she covered her face with her hands.

Then it seemed as if her prayers were being answered.

The shots became fewer.

The cannon still roared, but less often.

'We are sending them away,' she thought. 'Perhaps my prayers have helped them to do so.'

It seemed to her that a long time passed before the cannon fell silent. Gradually the rattle of the rifles slowed down.

But what did it mean?

'Where is he? Where is he?' she asked herself. 'Is he all right? Dear God, don't let him be hurt. Don't take him from me now, just when we have begun to find each other.'

Even as she was saying the last prayer from the depths of her heart, the door opened.

The light of the candles, which Venetia had left burning for him, showed her it was the Earl.

He pushed open the door with his hand. As she saw it was covered with blood, she gave a scream.

"You have been injured, you are hurt!" she cried.

"No, Venetia, truly I am unhurt."

"But you're bleeding. Oh God!"

"It isn't my blood. A man attacked me and I killed him."

"I'm glad," she said fervently. "I'm glad you killed him if he dared to attack you. I wish I had killed him myself."

"What a little warrior you are!" he said admiringly. "I'm safe now, my darling. They have started to withdraw. It's nearly over."

She burst into tears.

"There," he said, drawing her into his arms. "You have been so brave, and I'm proud of you. My darling, my darling – don't cry."

"I can't help it," she sobbed. "I love you so much and I was terrified in case I lost you."

He put his fingers under her chin.

"Did you say that you love me?" he asked in a tone of wonder.

"Of course I love you," Venetia whispered. "If you had died in the battle, I would have wanted to die too."

"My darling, my precious," the Earl said, "that's all I need to know. I have longed to tell you that I love you, but I didn't know how. I hardly dared to hope that you loved me."

"I have loved you for a long time," Venetia whispered, "but I was afraid of admitting it in case you didn't care for me."

"I have loved you from the first moment I saw you," the Earl told her. "But I wanted my wife, if I ever had one, to love me as much if not more than I loved her. Now at last I have found what I have been seeking."

They clasped each other in a long embrace. Then, suddenly they both stood still, listening, hardly daring to believe what they heard.

The guns were silent at last. The battle was over.

Soon it would be their time. Until then, Venetia could wait, knowing that now the wait would not be long.

*

There was no doubt about the victory. Not only had the British soldiers overcome their enemy, but they had taken several prisoners.

The following morning Venetia proved her worth again by helping the Colonel question them. There was no doubt that Kelton was the traitor, and had been promised a handsome payment for delivering his compatriots to the Russians.

"I am so grateful for your help," the Colonel said to her at last, "and now I can release you from active service. Devenish is recovering fast and can be our interpreter again.

The important thing now is for the two of you to return home and report on the situation to Her Majesty."

"I promise to tell her everything that has happened and to make her aware of your needs," the Earl said.

"I understand that Lord Anthony will not be travelling with you?" the Colonel enquired.

The Earl grinned.

"He has declared his intention of remaining here in India. He seems to think that life in England will not be exciting enough after all this."

"He's welcome to stay," Colonel Arkwright replied, also grinning. "He'll get bored after a while and then I'll send him home."

"I'll just wait for you to write your report," the Earl said, "and then we'll start the journey back to Bombay to board the ship for home."

On the next day they were ready to leave. Everyone turned out to see them off, including Anthony, now turned brown by the sun and full of the excitement of his new life.

"Goodbye, old fellow!" the Earl said. "I'll see you back in England some time, I dare say."

"I'm not sure you will," came the spirited riposte. "This life suits me."

"Goodbye, Anthony dear," Venetia said, and kissed him.

"I say!" he said.

Travelling first on horseback and then by rail, it took them three days to reach Bombay, where the ship was waiting.

"Let's depart as soon as possible," the Earl told the Captain. "We want to get home."

"Yes, my Lord."

In the years to come, Venetia was to remember that

voyage of love and happiness as one of the most exciting and thrilling times of her whole life.

The Earl loved her as she had always wanted to be loved, and in return she gave him the love he had told her he thought he would never find.

They were blissfully happy in their suite and seldom went anywhere else while they were on board.

"I love you, I love you," Venetia found herself saying over and over again.

The Earl's love for her seemed to increase every day they were at sea.

"I suppose I must admit that you did me a huge favour when you took Mary's place at the altar," he said to her once.

"Mary is a nice girl but I did not find her interesting. We would never have had a happy marriage. But you and I understand each other. We even share the same sense of humour and you will keep me fascinated all my days. My love, I could never, never find you boring."

"But perhaps I will be the bored one," she teased him.

"I shall have to make sure that you are not," he said, taking her into his arms.

As they neared home she said, a little sadly,

"I suppose that this has been our honeymoon. It seems to have slipped by as if it was flying."

"We are going to have a hundred honeymoons, the Earl told her. "But I think it is only right to return home first and give our report to the Queen, before we forget that anyone else exists in the world except two people who love each other as we do."

"While you are seeing the Queen, I'll go home and find out what's happened to Mary and David."

"I will hate every moment I am away from you," the Earl answered. "But I must not keep Her Majesty waiting for my report. You must come back to me quickly."

"I will do that," Venetia promised. "Because I too will be counting the minutes until I see you again."

"And then we'll continue our honeymoon and be even happier than we are now."

"I don't think that is possible," Venetia replied. "I am so happy and I love you with all my heart, in fact all of me does."

"And I love you with all of me," the Earl said, "and that is something I have never said to a woman before."

"I love you," Venetia whispered.

Then it was impossible to say any more.

She knew that her husband had his duty to do, but she still longed for the journey to last as long as possible.

But all too soon it came to an end. The ship docked, they took the train to London and on to Mountwood House in the heart of the most fashionable area.

Venetia was longing to see the house that would be her new home. She had heard of it as a magnificent residence, fit for noblemen. As the great doors swung open, she saw the whole staff gathered to welcome their new mistress.

When she entered, the housekeeper and all the maids curtsied and the butlers and footmen bowed low.

The butler rose and cleared his throat.

"Welcome to Mountwood House, your Ladyship," he said solemnly. "On behalf of all the staff, allow me to express the hope that you will be happy here."

She thanked him and took the Earl's arm to step over the threshold and be introduced to every member of the household. There were over a hundred of them, and she grew dizzy.

The last was a severe elderly lady with a rigid expression that barely concealed a look of anxiety. This was

Miss Angleton and the Earl had prepared Venetia to meet her.

"She was my mother's dresser," he had said. "After Mama died I kept her on because she had nowhere else to go, and she's always looked forward to my marriage so that she could dress another Lady Mountwood. The decision is yours of course – "

Looking now at Miss Angleton's face Venetia knew that she too would find her impossible to dismiss.

"I will rely on you to help me," she said, embracing her warmly. "You'll probably think I'm a little country mouse."

"You are Lady Mountwood," Miss Angleton said in a voice that settled all questions.

"I've never been put in my place so firmly," she chuckled to her husband over dinner that night. "But she took charge of my luggage very efficiently and had two maids scurrying around while she barked out orders."

"Only two?" he asked scandalised. "My mother had three. Four if it was a great occasion."

"Well, you can tell Miss Angleton that you think she isn't paying enough attention to my dignity," Venetia told him.

He shuddered.

"Heavens no! She terrifies me. Besides, she's already started to make you look like a Countess."

It was true. Miss Angleton had brushed Venetia's hair fiercely before taking out a pair of curling tongs and setting to work. The resulting creation was the last word in elegance and fashion.

"You are going to take your place in High Society, my darling," the Earl told her. "With your beauty and Miss Angleton's skill, you will take London by storm."

Venetia's eyes gleamed.

"I should like that," she said.

The following morning the Earl left the house early to see the Queen at Buckingham Palace, where she had moved, after leaving Windsor Castle.

Venetia caught the train to Fenway, the nearest town to her old home. There she hired a cab.

Everything seemed quiet as she drew up outside the house. But then she saw a curtain move upstairs and Mary's face was looking out.

Mary gave a shriek as she recognised her and came flying down to greet her.

"It's you, it's you," she cried. "You're really here at last. We wondered if we'd ever see you again."

She flung her arms about Venetia, who hugged her back, laughing. Then David appeared and stood looking bashful until the two women released each other and turned to him.

"This is David," Mary said proudly.

"I remember seeing you," Venetia said.

"But you haven't met properly before," Mary said. "Now he is my husband."

Venetia shook David's hand. Then she impulsively kissed him on the cheek, while Mary looked on, smiling with happiness.

Afterwards they all sat in the drawing room together, and Mary said,

"Tell us everything. What has happened to you?"

"Why, I married Lord Mountwood," Venetia said impishly. "But you knew that."

"Venetia!"

"And we went to India for our honeymoon and now we are home."

"But was he very angry when he found out?"

"He wasn't very pleased for a while," Venetia said, choosing her words carefully. "But we came to understand each other and now he's quite reconciled to having to put up with me."

"You mean he's madly in love with you?" Mary giggled.

Venetia just smiled.

"You're not going to tell me, are you?" Mary said.

"I will tell you that everything worked out for the best," Venetia said. "And that is all you need to know."

She smiled again, and there was something about her mysterious smile that told Mary everything.

"How have you managed here?" Venetia asked. "Has your father found out the truth yet?"

Mary exchanged a glance with David and replied,

"We've been very clever while you have been away. No one in my family knows we are here."

"But you have been happy?" Venetia enquired.

"We have been very, very happy," Mary answered, "and I have something else to tell you. David has set up a practice here and the local people are flocking to him."

"That's wonderful news," Venetia exclaimed.

"We are looking for a small house," Mary said, "so that we can live there and be independent. That's important, because I'm sure when Papa knows we are married he will be so furious that there will be no use asking him for any help."

"I rather suspected that," Venetia replied. "That is why I have a plan. I want you to stay here and live in this house. I won't be needing it for a while and I would not want my house to be used by anyone except you.

"I will only want it when my eldest son, if I have one, is married. Then I would like to think he would live here in the home which has belonged to my family for so many years."

Mary stared at her.

"Are you saying we can stay here?" she asked.

"Yes, that's what I'm saying."

"We would love to live here," Mary answered excitedly. "We have said over and over again how happy we have been, since we came straight from the wedding in through this front door."

"Well now I'm married to Ivan," Venetia replied, "I shall be living in his home."

"You mean homes," Mary said. "Everyone knows that he has Mountwood House in London and Mountwood Castle in the country, and that they are both extremely luxurious."

"Well, they could have been yours," Venetia said impishly.

"No, thank you," Mary said promptly. "You have a coronet, but I have David and he is worth more than anything."

David smiled, clearly finding this reply very acceptable.

"And I have something else just as important," Mary said excitedly. "I really am carrying a child and it's going to be twins. I have been longing to write and tell you about it, but I had to wait until you came home."

"I am absolutely delighted," Venetia replied. "I hope I can be a Godmother to both of them."

"That is exactly what I said to David," Mary answered with a laugh. "I believe that when Papa knows he will no longer be angry, but will simply want to enjoy his grand-children."

"I am sure he will," Venetia agreed. "I'm so pleased that you are as happy as I am."

"Are you really happy," Mary asked, "or are you just telling us so?"

Venetia smiled.

"I am telling you and it is the absolute truth that I have been blessed by God. I have found the man I love with all my heart and he loves me more than any woman has ever been loved before."

She spoke in a way which made Mary bend forward and kiss her.

"I am so very glad, darling," she said. "You have always been so wonderful to me. David says he blesses you every day for making it possible for us to marry each other."

"Then what more can we ask?" Venetia answered. "Now I must go back to London because my husband will be home soon and will be waiting for me. He has gone to see the Queen today and I am longing to hear how Her Majesty has reacted."

Mary's hands flew to her mouth.

"Oh, she will be so angry!"

"I don't think you should worry," Venetia said. "If she is angry, Ivan will talk her out of it using all his charm."

All the way home she was willing the train to move faster and take her back to her beloved.

To her delight she learnt as soon as she arrived, that the Earl was back from Buckingham Palace. She ran into the sitting room and the moment she opened the door, he held out his arms.

"You are back!" he exclaimed. "I was feeling worried in case I had lost you."

"You will never lose me," Venetia replied.

He kissed her as they sat on the sofa.

"I have missed you," she said. "What happened with the Queen?"

"I made my report and she was very pleased. Apparently Lord Lytton had already written to her to praise my wife. She says I'm very fortunate to have married such a brave and resourceful lady."

"But does she know exactly which lady you have married?" Venetia asked warily.

"I did tell her what had happened."

"Was she angry?"

"I am not quite sure," he said slowly. "She didn't say very much."

"Ivan how can you be so provoking? She must have said something."

"She said, 'well I never!' Then she said, 'well, well, well!' Finally she said, 'who would have believed it?' Oh yes, and she also added, 'I never heard of such a thing.'"

"But what does all that mean?"

"I think it means she's trying to decide whether she's angry or not. She wants me to return on Friday, taking you and both your friends to meet her."

Venetia's hands flew to her mouth.

"Then Mary was right. She said the Queen would send for them. I reassured her that that would not happen. Oh, whatever are we going to do?"

"We're going to obey the Queen," he said. "There is no question of doing anything else."

"I thought you could charm her out of her anger."

"You overestimate my charm," he said dryly. "Not everyone sees me through your eyes. The Queen likes to be obeyed."

"But her order is nonsensical."

He grinned.

"I hope I'm there when you tell her so."

"Oh, you're impossible."

"I suggest you invite Mary and David to London to stay with us for a couple of nights. Then we all can travel to the Palace together."

She despatched a letter the next morning, and on Thursday afternoon Mary and David, both extremely nervous, arrived at Mountwood House.

The huge Mountwood carriage was waiting for them, drawn by four white horses. In a few minutes they were on their way to Buckingham Palace.

As the magnificent gates opened to admit them, Mary became distinctly nervous, but the clasp of David's hand steadied her.

Venetia realised that she too was nervous. She tried not to show it, but she could not help twisting her hands together.

"Surely you're not scared?" Ivan teased her. "Is this the woman who took on the Russians?"

"The Russians were easy," she replied. "The Queen is another matter."

He laughed and drew her hand through his arm.

All too soon they were drawing to a halt, the steps were let down and they were admitted into the Palace.

There was a long walk down interminable corridors. Venetia told herself that she was worrying about nothing, but the fact was that she had defied Queen Victoria, the most formidable monarch in the world.

She pictured the Queen sitting aloof on her throne, looking down on them from a great height and hurling down thunderbolts of rage to annihilate them.

She would face it for herself, but she could not bear the thought that she might have harmed her beloved husband.

Then they were facing a pair of ornate double doors,

which were opened by two footmen.

"The Earl and Countess of Mountwood, and Mr. and Mrs. Windham, Your Majesty."

He stepped aside and Venetia received her first clear view of Queen Victoria.

She almost gasped at what she saw.

There was no sign of the fearsome monarch she had expected. Instead she saw a tiny woman of about sixty with a sad face and weary eyes. She was seated at a desk, gazing at a large picture that stood just in front of her.

It showed a very handsome young man, and Venetia recognised the late Prince Albert, the husband she had loved so devotedly and whose death, eighteen years earlier, had devastated her.

At last she looked up.

"So there you are, Ivan. And this is your wife. And this – " she indicated for Mary to approach, "this is the young woman who defied me."

"Oh, Your Majesty please do not be angry with me," Mary begged. "I didn't mean to defy you, but David and I were so much in love?"

"And you think love justifies you in disobeying your Queen, do you?"

Mary put her head up.

"Yes, Your Majesty. I do."

There was a frozen silence. Then the Queen's face broke into a smile.

"You are perfectly right. True love justifies any risk. When you have found it, you should fight to keep it, even if you have to fight the Queen herself. And the rewards of love are so great, you should seize them while you can."

But then her smile faded and she turned to Venetia.

"Come here."

Venetia approached, dropping into a deep curtsy.

"Your Majesty."

"You cannot claim to have been in love, since I gather you had never met him before you carried Ivan off."

The Earl stirred.

"Actually Your Majesty, I rather think it was I who carried her off."

"Nonsense, of course you didn't," the Queen said with unexpected robustness. "She made a complete fool of you. If I'd known you were so easily taken in, I would not have sent you to India."

"Yes, Your Majesty," he said meekly.

"So what have you got to say for yourself, young woman? You can't make love *your* excuse? Were you ambitious for his title?"

"Oh no, Your Majesty," Venetia said promptly. "I thought he needed improving and I decided I was the right person to do it."

Queen Victoria's lips twitched.

"Indeed? And do you think you have improved him?"

Venetia threw her husband a mischievous look before saying,

"I've made a start, but there's still much work to be done."

This time the Queen laughed out loud.

"Well, you're well placed to do it," she said. "He told me yesterday that he was madly in love with you. Has he ever told you that?"

Venetia blushed.

"Yes, Your Majesty. Many times."

"And he will tell you many times more, I think. Do you love him too?"

She blushed even harder.

"Yes, Your Majesty. With all my heart."

The Queen gave a little sigh.

"Then that is all that matters. I should never have ordered him to marry a stranger without love. I know, better than anyone, how vital love is and how sad life can be without it."

She cast a glance at the picture of Prince Albert, and for a moment the elderly woman vanished, replaced by the eager young bride who would love one man all her life, even when he was no longer with her.

"You are wise, all of you," the Queen said. "You know what is important."

Her voice grew suddenly husky as she said,

"I pray that you may be luckier than I was and have long lives together."

"Your Majesty," Venetia sighed, torn with sympathy.

"Go now!" the Queen commanded. "We will meet again and then we will talk more. You will find my wedding gifts to you on the table. Take them as you leave. Now go."

Their gifts, which they opened in the corridor outside, were exquisite pieces of porcelain from the Queen's collection. She herself had handwritten the message.

"She forgave us before we came here," Venetia exclaimed in wonder.

"Of course," her husband told her. "She will forgive anything for love. She understands the bond that unites us, my darling.

"And she has wished us the greatest gift – that we will share long lives together. That is my prayer too, that we shall always have each other, from now until the end of time."

"Until the end of time," Venetia murmured. "So much and so little to want. And as we have it, we have everything."

Mary and David had walked ahead of them and were standing in a corner, clasped in each other's arms. They joined Ivan and Venetia and the four of them walked out of the Palace, leaving behind the woman, their Queen, who had known love, lost it and found the strength to bless them.

In the radiance of that blessing, they emerged into the sunlight and saw that it streamed ahead of them all the way into eternity.